One for Sorrow

and other stories

ANTHONY GLAVIN

poolbeg press

With acknowledgements to *The Irish Press* 'New Irish Writing', *Best Irish Short Stories 3* and *Irish Heritage* where some of these stories first appeared.

This book is one of a series devoted to the modern Irish short story. Ireland's contribution to the short story is world famous, but much of the best work of the acknowledged masters and of the new hands is either out of print or has never been published in book form.

The aim of this series is to make that work generally available.

Contents

	Page
Kinnakillew Sunday	7
Bread Alone	22
Nettle Broth	41
Fables	61
Killing Time	78
One For Sorrow	90
Vanishing Boundaries	106
The Answer Man	118
Housebound	130
Of Saints And Scholars	140

First published 1980 by
Poolbeg Press Ltd.,
Knocksedan House,
Swords, Co. Dublin, Ireland.

© Anthony Glavin, 1980.
The generous assistance of An Chomhairle Ealaion (The Arts Council)
in the publication of this book is gratefully acknowledged.

Cover by John Dixon
Book designed by Steven Hope

Printed by Cahill Printers Limited,
East Wall Road, Dublin 3.

Kinnakillew Sunday

It was a spring evening at a rock quarry south of Boston when Liam finally laid hold of what had taken his uncle's life. Ten years after the fact, across deep water as his uncle had called America, a good deal of time and space to at last fathom a death by drowning off the Irish coast.

The outing was Lisa's idea, a swim in the quarry with another couple, followed by a picnic supper at the water's edge. Liam took his lunch hour to buy a swim suit, changing in the men's room at work. He put the trunks on under his trousers, placed his shorts in the Filene's bag which he then rolled up in his towel. As Lisa would bring food for them both, only to worry whether the clouds meant rain.

'Call the weather,' suggested an officemate of whom he inquired the forecast.

'Nothing but numbers,' Liam rang off in disgust. 'Probability of precipitation thirty per cent, relative humidity seventy-five,' he droned, mimicking the monotone of a Mary Boyle who sounded far more Boston than Irish. 'Sunshine and showers reduced to decimals.'

'At least we post odds here,' replied his colleague who had once spent a holiday in Ireland never to see the sun.

'Marine biology,' Liam said, describing his internship at the State Division of Fisheries to Arthur and Kathy in the back seat as Lisa turned onto the Southeast Expressway. She had picked him up first, outside the office building just off Government Center, surprising him with a quick kiss beside his ear. 'Bread and water,' was all she would tell him as he shifted the wicker hamper into the luggage space behind the back seat.

'Better that than bread and quicksilver,' he came back, though handy enough should one of them be late to supper. All in jest, without a thought to the uncle.

'And yourself, Arthur?' Liam now asked, eager to deflect the conversation as he often was with strangers.

A consultant, Arthur answered, a job description peculiar to the States which never failed to evoke Delphi and the oracle for Liam. 'For a small computer outfit in Charlestown.'

Possibly it was this crowd that distorted the weather. Or divined rather, reading tapes and memory banks like the entrails of any eagle. Only he was thinking out of both sides of his mouth now, for didn't they fish with computers as well, charting the catch of cod off George's Banks. He left the weather out of it, left Arthur to do most of the talking, adding only that he knew shark's oil to be prized as a computer lubricant. Kathy, it turned out, worked in a camera shop.

Half an hour later Lisa turned them down a dirt road, following it through woods which soon thinned to a marsh on their left. The opening was oddly clear of reeds and brush, the only vegetation a field of skunk cabbage which commanded the swamp. Leaf-green, they appeared to have burst full-grown through the black mud itself, their image remaining with Liam like a photograph along the road which ended at the quarry.

Leaving the car they picked their way down a trail to the bottom where they looked into a canyon of sorts, shaped by granite walls which rose forty feet above the water at the opposite end. Moments after they reached the water, Liam found himself at sea. Leaving him yet half-clad, the others had stripped off and leapt in from a table-like rock. The new suit now but further embarrassment, he removed it in one motion with his trousers, seeking the quarry waters like so much bedclothing to pull over himself. A fine figure of a biologist he made, afraid of the naked body—before the freezing water took thought away.

The other three had struck off separately, so he swam to his right, the fourth point on the star or compass. When in Rome or Boston he told himself—until a memory of his first meeting Lisa made him laugh, his present plight perhaps nothing but inevitable.

They had been seated a few yards apart at the fountain in Copley Square, one of the first warm days that spring. Entirely aware of the young woman in a skirt the colour of daffodils, he spoke only as she removed sandals to soak her feet in the fountain pool. 'I'd a notion to cool mine,' he told her, 'only I wasn't sure . . .' He left the sentence hanging, letting his accent explain his uncertainty as he bent down to slip off shoes and stockings.

They had begun then by unclothing. Though in the city centre, something intimate and daring in it all the same, at least to his Irish self. She took a cigarette from him, not without hesitating. A hint here again of something almost illicit, quickly dispelled. 'I'm trying to quit,' she explained, the flat American accent belying all intrigue.

'There was a fountain in Indianapolis when I was little,' she told him after they had talked some of Ireland. 'At night its spray had every kind of colour. Lit by floodlights. My grandmother said the colours came from people having washed their feet there during the day.' She seemed as interested in the pool as in himself, staring down at her naked feet. Maybe it was narcissus, the colour of her skirt, as if he had missed a clue.

'Are you from Indianapolis?' he asked after a while, somewhere to do with racing cars he knew.

'From a crossroads sixty miles north,' she had said, now making him consider, neck deep in water, that a rural childhood might be much of the reason that they got on well. Though Lisa might well think his own in Donegal downright rustic. Their first date had been a day-trip to the Berkshires where they searched for sassafras, Lisa teaching him to identify the saplings by their mittenlike leaves. Biologist or no, a fish out of water in a Massachusetts woods. They made tea from the roots at Lisa's flat. Apartment she called it, though actually it was little more than a bed-sitter, a small alcove serving as scullery. 'Kitchen,' she corrected him as he carried the cups to the sink.

There was little rural about the digs he had left

in Dublin. A privet hedge fronted the terraced house on Sandycove Road where he had taken a room to be near the sea. Only a few minutes walk from the Martello Tower, it was forty minutes by bus into the city centre. Departing Donegal first for the University, he had then accepted a job with the Ministry of Fisheries. Having more or less adjusted in five years to city life, he still encountered an occasional cross-current in what had once seemed entirely strange waters; at times a kind of tension between training and experience, as though theory and language could obscure, attentuate the actual—much as computers had done to the weather in America. If he knew bluestone as copper sulphate now, there remained a loyalty to the memory of his father scattering the blue powder on new thatch; to keep the rot off, turning it golden in the bargain. Not a posture common to all who came up from the country, it was shared at least by one friend there, a technician with the Ministry of Agriculture who sought out the seventh son of a seventh son—having spent weeks treating a case of cattle scab with ointments to no avail. In two days his arm cleared, either the cure or the salve having finally taken. Not entirely at ease with moves he had made, it seemed to Liam as good a time as any to try America for a year.

She was at university herself Lisa told him at the fountain. Finishing a doctorate in Italian painting though teaching positions were nowhere to be found. 'A kind of Irish practicality in that,' he told her, adding despite her laugh that he meant no offence at all. They had seen each other for the next month then, excursions to the country, cinema, and theatre where she had charmed him afterwards, idly chewing on a string of pearls as they sat over coffee. There was about her a certain coolness which intrigued him, one almost more of colour than of temperament, there despite the reds and yellows she favoured, her scalp almost pink from the sun beneath the light blonde hair. At the same time he sensed an intimacy between them, something beyond the kiss or two they had shared. But nothing that added up—in his experience, anyhow— to this quarry evening.

They were treading water now, only yards apart, commenting on its chill. Deflected by the water her breasts looked no larger than his own. Suspended there, Liam realized it was indeed his own experience that mattered here, for never in Ireland had he seen a woman naked whom he had never bedded. In fact he doubted his father had ever seen his mother so—even after marriage, the two of them from a village on the Donegal coast where it would be a rare sight to see a couple on the road. Sundays his family had strung out for half a mile on the way to Mass. His father first, Liam and his brothers at scattered intervals, his mother bringing up the rear to the Church where men and women sat by sex on opposite sides of the aisle.

If Dublin were different, America had proved altogether something else. There seemed women everywhere, their street dress as the warm weather came much like what one might see at Killiney beach south of Dublin on an August day. Mornings Liam drove early to work, along the Fenway enclosed by dark green trees, often a mist hanging like smoke above the road. Most of those about at that hour were nurses at either end of their shifts, moving down footpaths beneath the trees like figures in a fantasy. If Donegal were not without its sensuousness, it was for Liam of an unpeopled sort: the black sheen of rain-soaked stone or moonlight spilt on a turf shed floor, that of a landscape where no one moved through the morning like these forms in white.

They were now swimming together, paralleling one another with a slow side-stroke that maintained the few yards between them like a tacit neutral zone. Or neutered zone he thought, acutely aware of his body whether it was his nakedness or the cold. The sensation reminded him of bathing in the cottage as a child; doling out the kettle into the basin he would in his mind divide his body along dotted lines, like those on the butcher's chart in Donegal Town.

'They dive sometimes from that ledge,' Lisa said, breaking her stroke to point at an outcropping some twenty feet above them.

'Not unless I had to,' Liam answered, thinking it took one fear to vanquish another, the chill of the quarry waters mattering little once he stood without a stitch. And at that he remembered his uncle.

That a man over sixty in Kinnakillew went swimming at all was unusual of itself. Many swam as lads, few did so after they turned twenty-five. Or after they married, as if having learned a new rhythm for the body they no longer would unclothe. Still, his uncle, a bachelor, swam Sundays in the summer months. Waiting for the football game to empty the strand, he would fold his clothes neatly on· the sand, walk out to the waist of his black bathing togs before diving under.

There was no game that Sunday however, and several women were among the parties seated on the sand despite a dull day, the clouds low but little moisture in the air. Liam was among the youngsters dossing about on the football field when the alarm first sounded from the sea. Across the expanse of sea grass which backed the strand came the cries for help, sounding like frightened daws. Racing toward the water Liam saw a knot of men up the south side of the bay. They were gesturing at a figure in the water below, waving him toward the strand and away from the rocks on which they stood. Able to surmise that the sea had sprung up, the wind having come round, what Liam could not grasp was how the very man who had taught him to read the sea was now attempting the rocks with their treacherous wash, surely knowing to try for the strand. 'Should you ever go overboard, save your strength and use the waves against the wind,' Uncle Dinny had cautioned upon first taking him on the water, the two of them rowing out one morning after mackerel.

'A group of us used to go skinny-dipping in high school,' Lisa spoke. 'At a reservoir on the opposite side from the public beach.' Having reached the far end they rested for a moment, clinging to the quarry wall. The water here was as black as the rock, her body white beneath its surface like a mirror-image of his own, startling him with its similarity to his slight and light-boned self. 'There were just girls but we always waited until night.'

'I fear we never did anything quite so daring,' Liam said, offering little in return. If his confusion at being left half-clothed upon the rock afforded any clue, it seemed to show him trapped in a perpetual adolescence, still sitting down to that crazy salad of shame and delight which the body held. A kind of Irish heritage it seemed, one that would have him ever waiting for night to fall. Should he tell her how at school sometimes in Ballyshannon they had bought *The Irish Times*, smuggling it into the dormitory where they read aloud the list of books banned by the censorship board. *Beyond the Mini-Skirt* and *Twice Nicely*, though he could not be sure now that these were not titles they had fashioned on their own, inspired by the Dublin daily. In the third year they heard Brother Michael tell of the couple in the parked auto, a high wind toppling a tall tree at the moment the lad unbuttoned the lass's blouse, the two of them crushed dead in mortal sin. To Liam that same spring there seemed nothing more alluring than the girls in white bound for confession in the evening, his guilt compounded by coveting those on their very way to speak with God. If deterred at all by Brother Michael, in the last year some of the lads had gone so far as to adventure along the river bank, though few claimed to have outstripped their dead predecessor in the auto, high wind or not.

His second year in Dublin he moved from the University to digs near the distillery. If by now he had his doubts, it seemed the Church did as well, challenging Patrick and disclaiming doctrine—leaving Liam to scrawl 'Locate the Limbo Millions' in the Gents whenever he was jarred. 'You're trying to do me,' suggested Mary of the long hair behind the shop counter beneath his flat, holding out the coins he had proffered for a bag of crisps. Not that I wouldn't mind he thought, fumbling, flustered, for the proper change. And hadn't he too, after a time and a great deal more fumbling between them on the old settee, whenever he could talk her up and his room-mate out. 'I was afraid because I was naked so I hid'—from Genesis to Stephen D., a worn out Irish story, there beneath their laughter in Kinnakillew at the village doctor so shy it was said he would deliver only baby boys. And as he understood this evening, there like a current beneath the bay the day his uncle died.

Those nearest the water could hear him say how hard it was to grab hold—until the wash ended the struggle, dashing him against the rocks to crack his brow. It was not until they put in a boat and came round to retrieve his body however, that they saw why he had ignored their counsel to try for the strand.

'He'd swum the bay twice,' Liam's father told his mother that afternoon, 'resting on the sand-bar as he usually did. Likely it was there that he lost his togs.'

'But to drown?' she offered into her husband's silence.

'Not wanting to come in on the strand where there were people, with himself exposed, he tried for the rocks on this side,' his father finished. At three o'clock the clouds broke, driven off by the same wind which had turned the sea against his uncle, sunlight now flooding the bay as if to belie the drowning not an hour before. The next morning they found the suit itself, there in the trail of flotsam left by the tide: kelp, pieces of turf, bottle corks, a sheep's jaw and a battered kettle.

Still the same sea which claimed his uncle had offered Liam a way out of Kinnakillew, the sea and all Dinny had taught him of it before his death. 'Mad as he is for the water, the man's a gull,' Liam's father would complain, resentful perhaps of the brother's growing influence on his son. 'You'll see that the lad does no chores at all,' he would chide on evenings in October as the two of them returned long past milking, coming up the meadow in the gathering dark from the rocks below. It was these fall nights with Dinny that Liam remembered best, angling into the filling tide as the wind tight from the east went to the bone itself, freezing his hands so that the warmth of the fish gurry came always as a surprise when they gutted their catch in a tidal pool.

'It wasn't on,' Dinny would tell his brother when they returned empty-handed, though Liam might have learned that night to read an approaching storm from the manner in which the plentiful fish had refused to take. 'Just tumbling on the fly, just tumbling,' his uncle's complaint. Young seal crying were another sign of bad weather. Mackerel were scavengers; herring the cleanest there were, eating nothing but the soil of the sea.

Like most in the village he put in potatoes, a few onions, but Dinny had scant use for the land. If the rocky soil had been always worthless he told Liam, there was once a time when fishing was all. 'Why a lad with a length of herring net, thirty fathoms just, would get himself a wife sooner than your man with forty acres.' It was as much as he ever said on the subject of women. The great schools of cod disappeared after the war, however; the herring no longer dependable; the sea serving more often to escape the barren land in passage to Liverpool or Stranraer than to Dublin as Liam had done. 'An Irishman's drowned in the canal, and all's well,' the Glasgow watch had cried at night according to his uncle's story.

They had waked Dinny in their own cottage. If not to avoid the task it would have been to make decent his own dwelling, then to spare the mourners the mile walk up the glen. A master on the sea, the man had proved a disaster by his hearth, the chimney never managing more than a part of the smoke from the range. On a bright day the interior remained clear enough, but with dampness it grew a kind of misty within, the chair as likely as not to rise with the visitor, stuck to the arse of his pants. The room was covered with soot; the bread stored inside a trunk tasted yet of smoke.

'Shall we eat?' asked Lisa, gesturing at the other two who were now standing on the rock.

'I'd say we've earned it,' Liam said as they started back. Halfway across the quarry he felt the even colder current from a spring strike his side, like the draught from an open door. Slipping through to the wake again, he saw it was his father's response to Dinny's death that he remembered more clearly than even his own feelings at the time, as if his father's grief had at last sanctioned the love that Liam had held. 'It wants eating,' his mother had coaxed, offering the plate of Madeira to her husband who, having extinguished half a dozen cigarettes between forefinger and thumb, sat rubbing the fingers as though they were the source of his bewildering pain. Refusing the sweetbread he turned to a neighbour and began a story Liam had never heard before.

'We were down together one evening after glasán. I was leaping from one rock to another when my pole caught in a crevice, dumping me in. "Grab my pole," I hear Dinny saying so I did. I minded not knowing how to swim less than I did the sea-wrack which rose in the water about my head. Cautioning me not to break the pole, Dinny fished me out.'

'He was angry with you,' stated a neighbour who had only older brothers.

'He kicked me hard in the stomach,' his father replied, 'to take the fright off me he said, adding it was small odds to him if I wished to go swimming clothed.' The story led to others of mishaps on the water, one concerning two brothers who had put out one morning in a dinghy. The boat overturned and only one man survived. 'God saved ye,' they told him in Irish when he came onto the strand. 'It was only the great struggle I made myself saved me,' the man spat out as he lay gasping upon the sand. A decent man, the storyteller added, no blackguard, but hard with a terrible temper, leaving Liam to puzzle why God had let his uncle die.

'That was cold enough to wake you up,' observed Arthur as they dressed upon the rock. 'Cold enough to wake you,' echoed Kathy with a grandmother from Cavan as it turned out, making the joke for Liam's sake as though she had read his mind. Or else there was nothing like nakedness to suggest mortality he decided. Fear of nudity but a fear of death as psychology argued, his uncle trapped there in the sea, sink or swim—without a tinker's chance. Acting the Irish Paddy, he came back at Kathy with the story of the Yank who witnessed his third Irish funeral in as many days. 'Do they die often here?' came the enquiry. 'No, only the once,' a farmer replied. Glancing at Lisa in the failing light he saw the white of her undergarments like a bird at dusk. Or was he only here aping Daedalus again, the trace of her breast under the heavy sweater like a promise of spring beneath its bulky knit. Sitting down to supper they managed all but the blueberry cheesecake before the rain began.

Liam saw his uncle as clearly twice after the evening at the quarry. First was in a dream where Dinny stood high on a mountain over a bog lake above the glen. He was casting a line into the lake, filling Liam with worry that he would be unable to do the same, for the gear would surely foul on the heather before it even cleared the reeds along the water's edge. The dream then shifted, leaving his uncle on the mountain but Liam now racing down the strand after a giant balloon which trailed its gondola along the sand.

The second was a month later, the evening he and Lisa turned lovers. They had spent the week-end on Cape Cod, and Liam could feel its sand along the sheets on which they lay, her leg resting over his. The flood within his brain receding slowly, he saw a series of images pass before his eyes without rhyme or reason: a rabbit entirely skinned hanging from the byre door, the wind rippling water standing in a sheep-dip tank, the first edge of ash like frost on turf still black upon the fire.

And then his uncle on the day he died. Not as they had pulled him from the water, all phlegm and blood running down his face, but floating face down with his arms outflung, the fine moss lace upon his limbs, rising and falling on the gentle swell like an outsized jellyfish, his body pale in the black water as if a reflection of clouds. Matching the movement of the water with Lisa's breathing, he watched his uncle floating there, lulled by the very motion, until he sank like a stone into sleep.

Bread Alone

Since summer it was obvious in Glenmore that Colum Boyle had become worse about the mountain. He came no more often into the pub, but once there with drink taken, he invariably got onto gold.

'Beautiful Butte,' he would begin, twisting his head on its long neck from side to side. Sometimes he also twirled his hands, all the while regarding them with a slight air of amazement, as if they belonged to somebody else. 'Beautiful Butte, though it's nothing but copper there.'

His faith in buried wealth was nothing new. Dating from the day his father returned from Montana, it was nearly of an age with Colum who was somewhere over seventy. Yet always capable of embroidering a border of self-parody around his speculations, a satiric edge which coloured not just himself but the village also, a margin that seemed since summer to have disappeared.

'You want copper for electricity, but gold is the international standard of values.' Playing his theme like a fishing pole, he was not so frequently in the pub that no one would rise to the bait.

'Times have changed, Colum. It's all Deutschmarks at the moment,' said Peter McGinty, surfacing from a deep pool in a corner of the pub. 'I've a yen for your mark, as the Japanese told the German.' A ripple of laughter suggested Peter had slipped the hook. No doubt knowing of what he spoke, first man in the Glen to have sold a building site to a German visitor.

'The dollar is still official currency,' Colum said, 'and the dollar is backed by gold,' trying the shallows at the far end of the bar.

'A new dollar any more, Colum, a Petro-dollar,' the fly having drifted on the current a moment before Francy Gara struck.

To Colum on a good night they were like the black pollock which followed the filling tide in lumps, turning the sea to silver as they broke the surface in frenzied pursuit of a bit of wool. You wanted the right wind, though; else they would not take, only just tumble on the fly.

'Gold's got little to do with it this weather,' continued Francy. ''Less it's black gold. Oil's what you want these days.' Whereas they once left Donegal to work the Scottish harvest, it was now employment off the Scottish coast, on platforms in the North Sea where wages were beyond belief. What was more, at home that summer ships to do with exploration of Irish waters had anchored within sight of the small pier two miles from the village.

'You saw the boats yourself the year,' McGinty baited Colum in turn.

'I haven't seen the sea these five years,' said Colum, laughter adhering to the line like wee shreds of seaweed to fishing gut. 'The only oil in those waters is what you get from a shoal of mackerel.'

Casting into memory, he saw his father wave him further up the banks above the pier—to look for any slick upon the sea. 'Sure the black-back gull will find oil sooner than any ship.'

'When was it you got worse than you were,' Francy Gara asked of the good nights, more truth than jest to the inquiry of late, good nights or not. Switched on to talk of minerals, Colum would drift off into himself as they turned to the poor turf that year, whether Banners could be grown in clay, once more to mark a returning tide of bitterness which seemingly consideration of metals could alone hold back. It seldom overflowed into venom or spleen, however, even with too much drink. Nibbling on his pipe in a chair by the fire, Colum, unlike some others, rarely annoyed. Connie Meehan, for instance, who late that night opened his mouth wide, displaying the only gold he held there to be in all Glenmore. Though it was but Fool's Gold of a kind, Colum had not thought to tell Connie that until he was home in bed.

He rose late the next morning, the cold weather having come on in the past fortnight, bringing his rheumatism with it. He was worst with it mornings, needing to jerk himself stiffly about like a cat rising from its nap. Out the door for turf he glanced at the mountain several hundred yards beyond the road which ran below the cottage.

'There's gold in Glenmore right enough, but it's in that mountain, not in the park at all.' So spoke his father the morning he returned from America, addressing Colum's grandfather as if the old man were not five years dead. Lowering his gaze to the park, little more than a long enclosed meadow below the cottage, Eamonn the Miner had looked into memory at the haphazard mounds of soil excavated by three brothers, under the direction of a father consumed by belief there was gold below. They had found nothing of value, earning only the nicknames of Eamonn, Sean and Watty the Miner.

Some fifteen years later Eamonn the Miner hired on with Anaconda in America. Schooled at the copper company in Butte, he conversed of alloys and ingots upon his return. To Colum at first it might have been simply soup his father was on about, all carrots and bullion until the mystery of mining language eased somewhat. Gold leaf proved elusive for a time as well, if only there being few leaves of any kind about Glenmore to survive the salt blown off the sea. When vocabulary was no longer a problem, Eamonn the Miner set Colum and his brother Michael lessons on placer and lode gold. The latter what their father and uncles would have uncovered digging to a depth in the park, had the grandfather Andrew struck it rich. 'We'd have found China sooner than our fortunes there,' their father told them, his own father's misplaced faith like the disputed article between two Presbyterian sects.

In fact Eamonn the Miner had returned from Montana a proselyte to placer gold, converted to alluvial deposits found along stream beds. 'Gold is six times as heavy as other metal,' he informed his sons, pointing at the stream which descended the eastern slope. The bedrock where its waters crossed their far meadow was possibly the richest soil in Donegal.

Nor was it done by deduction alone. If only out

of rebellion against his father's obsession with the park, Eamonn the Miner had long suspected the mountain. Before sailing to America he filled a matchbox with gravel from its lower slopes. Arranging in Butte for its analysis, he received months later a document certifying deposits of metallic lead, copper, silver, and a small percentage of gold. Eamonn the Miner sewed the certificate into the lining of his coat, stolen a year later on the train to New York for the boat home. Without the written proof he told no one of the gold in Glenmore but his wife and sons.

It was without mining Montana or park that his elder son had kept up the family concern, amassing from childhood on odd scraps and crumbs of mineral lore. Thin sheets of gold were translucent, transmit a green light he had read somewhere, encouraging Colum summers whenever the grassy slopes opposite seemed to glow in the last of the sun. By November however, little green remained, now encouraging but a few sheep who flecked the reddish bracken where they grazed two-thirds the distance up.

Colum stood in the thin sunlight, wishing it were warmer. At his feet nettle and mint unsheltered by the fuchsia were edged in black, mourning the summer. Within a week the fuchsia hedge itself would be sered by the wind. To his right a flock of crows flew over the Maguire's holding, all of them giving directions. Small wonder Andrew Boyle had prospected solely in the park his grandson decided, the corresponding land at James John Maguire's boasting the mine shaft which had put gold into every head. At the turn of the century English sappers had followed a course up Maguire's lane, begun a shaft not ten feet from the byre door. Long since overgrown, the shaft had covered an area thirty feet square, dug grave-depth six feet under.

'Is There Gold in These Hills of Donegal?' queried the county newspaper as next door Andrew Boyle set his sons to explore the meadow above the road. The mining operation at Maguire's lasted a fortnight, James John and two others hired to dig the earth, paid off weeks later without further word. Still the newspaper story brought a varying assortment of mineral men to Maguire's door. A geology student from Oxford inscribed rocks with yellow chalk, bringing his mother with him on a second visit. Another English, a painter on holiday, divined the course the sappers had followed with his hands clasped behind his back. 'Whatever it is, it's too wide for water,' he told the assembled watchers.

Within a few years Maguire died and the cottage was closed. Shortly after the funeral Colum's grandfather surprised three men in trench coats at the mouth of the shaft, a clocklike instrument at their feet. Pocketing the mechanism they left without a word. By then considered to be badly doting, Andrew Boyle could find no one else who had seen strangers about that day.

As a child Colum had watched the unhurried decay of Maguire's roof, the sods collapsing here and there to leave gaping holes, like mouthfuls bitten from the thatch. Looking back he felt they had done nothing right at Maguire's shaft. You wanted science and technology, not dowsers, to get out gold. He knew that much from his father who had returned from a land where miracles were wrought by those very means. Scientific rationalism the bedrock of his faith in the mountain, the gibes of the Connie Meehans mattered little, issuing forth as they did from ignorance.

He could remember yet a day the elder Meehan had struck young Connie for placing a piece of white quartzite into the stone ditch they were mending. A 'gentle' rock, much favoured by the faeries, it was seldom used in construction of any kind. Had not the priest said prayers over a large outcropping of quartz on the sea road where several parishioners had been troubled by the apparition of a woman. The prayers took, fixing her into the rock, and that was that.

It was more in auriferous quartz that the elder Boyle believed, flecked with visible grains of gold. Led into temptation by Eamonn the Miner, young Colum had risked what he felt to be sure trespass against his Heavenly Father, peeling off one afternoon a slice of the white rock from where it had begun to scale. He uncovered no signs of gold or woman, only a certain surprise to find the reverse of the immaculate chip all brown and green with moss and mould.

No doubt there was something to the old beliefs years back, perhaps a greater efficacy to prayer as well. No doubt dowsing revealed water—except you wanted it done with a proper hazel wand, not some English artist with his hands behind him like a prisoner on the march. And Eamonn the Miner himself forbade the flowering whitethorn within the cottage, thereby intimating that such things as 'gentle' might indeed exist. But most of it Colum had never given in to, superstitions only. And none of it would lead to gold. Explaining that gold-bearing quartz was worked a mile and a half below the surface, Colum would hear Francy Gara insist that by tunnelling each into the high banks on either side of the bay, communication could be established once they reached the proper depth. No less likely than their chances of communicating across the bar Colum would decide, giving it up in disgust. For all their refusal to credit his claims for the mountain, they offered him little data, few facts in return.

The young might know better but they knew nothing. Bereft of the old beliefs, their ignorance was up to date, making them all that more impoverished of knowledge to Colum who no less than the next man was capable of having it both ways. The nephew, Denis Michael, was a perfect example. Not thirty, he had worked in America for a year, maintenance man in a motel where they wagered on the number of drowned moles they would skim off the swimming pool mornings before the guests arose. Having spent a few hours in Butte between buses, Dinny returned to tell his uncle of the jet fighter set like a piece of statuary in the public park. It meant little to Colum who had never seen any plane closer than the chalk they inscribed across the sky, added little to a picture of Butte built around the photograph of a small frame house ('My room behind that window,' his father pointed) sliding into another house down a hill. To climb that hill to the pit of a winter's morning was in itself a day's work, according to his daddy.

Home from America Denis Michael turned to fishing, putting his savings toward an old half-decker. 'The leaves do not fall far from the tree,' his uncle informed the pub, his brother Michael, the lad's father, having spent more hours about the water than in the Glen. Summers Colum himself had fished, from a broad flagstone which sloped into the sea—until one August evening when a bound in the filling tide swept the ocean over the rock, pouring into his wellingtons. Braced against the backwash, he felt simultaneously with the icy water inside his stockings a strong urge to urinate, as if out of sudden confluence with the sea itself. Unnerved by the suck and swallow of mother ocean, Colum fled the rock. Yet had he forsworn the sea that evening, it would seem twenty years later little more than another token of that faith in the mountain, like a vow of poverty undertaken in hope of a greater reward across the road.

The nephew was first of two visitors to find Colum dozing off that afternoon beside the range. Dull and heavy after the dinner: another sign of age.

'Cold day,' Colum said, shifting to the window.

'Aye, cold day, but an east wind settles the water.'

Taking the vacated chair Denis Michael rubbed his hands before the open grate.

'Have you been out?' his uncle asked.

'Not since Tuesday. The sea's not right.'

'No herring then.'

'No herring worthwhile,' Denis Michael agreed, looking over at the old man. In the watery sunlight flecks of dried phlegm shone like scattered fish scales along the soiled cloth of his uncle's coat. An old man alone took no good care of himself, living on pan loaf and Stork margarine. Worse yet was an old man in an old shack, a sheet of newspaper at his back in bed against the cold. His mission having suggested itself, Denis Michael rigged his hand-line.

'They say McGinty got a wild amount off the German.'

'Either that or less,' Colum said, making out he hadn't heard lure and lead striking the water overhead.

'£2000 I heard.'

'Talk is cheap, if nothing else.'

'And silence is golden, I suppose,' came back the nephew, as surely as his father might have countered the older brother. A leaf off the tree, as Colum would tell the pub.

'There's gold in it, Dinny. That land is worth a thousand times whatever McGinty got.'

'There's money to be made all right,' the younger man shook his head. 'But it's in building sites, mind you, not mining rights.'

'You know nothing!'

'You haven't to sell the entire acreage,' Denis Michael said, paying out a little slack. No need to foul the line in the heavy wrack of the old man's stubbornness. 'A few sites across the road is all. You'd have money and more. You could put up a bungalow anywhere here in the park,' indicating with his hand the enclosed meadow long since gone to ragwort and rushes.

'Sure I've a great need for new digs at my age,' Colum said, the Glasgow slang to show he was not all Donegal, even if he had never left.

'You'd be warmer winters, sure you would. And

a few neighbours won't do any harm, either.'

'I'd need to learn German first,' the old man retorted, pleased to discover there was sport in being angled as well as angler. He wondered had his nephew heard of the Glen man who asked a visitor from Munich whether they spoke much German at home. Or was it only the native tongue in rural pockets, like Irish in the Gaelteacht, all English elsewhere? Colum liked to fancy it had been Connie Meehan, opening his mouth wide once more to display his ignorance.

'There's a Yank on holiday who's looking for a site,' Denis Michael said, shifting slightly in his seat as he set the hook.

Colum looked at his nephew as if the lad had produced a rubber eel all colours of the rainbow, a pot of gold at either end.

'From California, I believe,' Dinny added, gathering up line all the while.

He was asleep again when the knock sounded. Wondering what shower of bastards this time, he moved slowly to the door, taking it back as it opened onto Father Enright. Whereas the priest paid an annual visit to every household in the parish, Colum to keep things equal called on the Sacraments once a year. It scarcely seemed another twelve months gone, but there you had old age again. Like a bloody disease.

In fact Father Enright was early, having asked after the old man of Denis Michael at Bingo the week before.

'He's come down a lot, Father,' the fisherman said.

'Is it illness?'

'Not unless it's gold fever,' Dinny wanted to reply. He did not, and he said nothing about building sites either, knowing there would be no chance if the uncle thought he had put the priest onto him. 'He's getting on in years, Father.'

'He's gone on gold is what I should have said,' he told his wife in the car. 'Gone underground. Like a mole, he is, burrowing into that mountain.'

If only from having served in California where the war effort saw a shortage of priests as well as petrol, Father Enright got on with Colum. That he missed the gold rush of '49 by almost a century mattered not as the two men traded stories: the priest of the fruit-growing valleys worked by Mexicans; Colum of everything he had ever heard about Montana. When one afternoon the talk returned across deep water to settle on the mountain, the priest had mildly chided Colum. 'Render unto Caesar what is Caesar's,' he cited, regretting it at once.

'It's what belongs to the Lord that I'm on about, Father,' came Colum's reply.

'It's in that earth yet, and none of it minted,' the words sounding strangely like prayer, a profession of faith echoing in their insistence. 'Else how could He justify such land?' seemed the old man's plea, godforsaken rock pushing like ribs through soil so thin it was an insult. Another world to Arabia where you got oil by stepping in the wrong place.

The priest who was not a dull man caught some of this in Colum's tone. He was not a jealous man either, quite capable of distinguishing a Golden

Calf from a golden mountain. At the risk of rendering unto his parishioner's obsession he ministered unto what he sensed was need.

'Gold is the first metal mentioned in the Old Testament,' Father Enright offered in amends. ' "The gold of this land is pure: bdellium and onyx are found there." '

Colum nodded at the priest as if he could not have put it better himself. Apparently gold as it exists outside Havilah is rarely pure.

'I won't take tea, Colum,' the priest objected as the old man rose to rinse out the pot.

'You'd take stronger, Father, were there any in the house,' Colum said, wishing he had something to pour into the two china egg cups he kept for such occasions. Unable to locate the dishrag he hoped the day-old milk had not gone off as well. Poking into the small cupboard above the sink he found the last of a package of digestive biscuits; these he placed on a plate along with several slices of the pan loaf spread with lemon marmalade.

On this occasion the visit ran its course along lines of what they both chose to avoid. The priest did not quote Genesis and Colum, as badly doting as they thought him in the pub, made no attempt to verify a story current there: of the Irish wolfhound who was practically Father Enright's sole concession to earthly goods. According to Connie Meehan the dog, which by nature should bury bones, had got it backwards, partially uncovering the contents of a grave while digging in sanctified ground. Although Meehan said the priest had sent the hound away, Connie was as likely as any dog to get things the wrong way around.

It was not the only story of recent weeks to suggest a compulsion past Colum's own to take from the ground. The theft of Charlie Chaplin's body had been lately in the news. 'It was a Swiss plot,' someone told Colum in the pub, having confused the Lausanne cemetery with the perpetrators who were apparently a Pole and a Bulgarian. Whenever his films played years back at the schoolhouse, Colum had paid an admission for both evenings. Learning only from the actor's obituary of *Gold Rush*, one of several Chaplin films never to make it as far as Glen.

The wolfhound was not the only topic which Colum left alone. More than once he found himself wanting to confess something — not annoy the priest with the feeble sins of an old man, but tell of the certificate from the Montana mine. Like his father before him Colum had never told a soul. Sorely tempted, he held his tongue, troubled by a memory of his grandfather's three gentlemen in trench coats with a clocklike gadget.

Maybe the mountain wanted a Californian, he considered after the priest departed. Sure there had been nothing but English at Maguire's shaft, and what had come of it? Nothing, just. Nor was this the uninformed bigotry of his grandfather Andrew, attributing the haze which followed an east wind to factory smoke blown over from Birmingham. More a bias based upon facts, the English to Colum's mind having done little in the line of technology since Watt and steam.

Stopping halfway to the byre he rubbed his hands together, then tucked them into his armpits. The east wind which settled his nephew's sea brought frost as well, though it would be early in the season for that. For years he had worried about frost: too much, too soon, and any turf still wet upon the bog would crack until it crumbled. Away to dust like straw which rats have chewed. Ashes to ashes, dust to dust he chanted to himself. Gold dust and gold dollars. Another day, another dollar as they said in Butte.

One would find rats in turf also, but unlike with straw they did little destruction here. All the same he had helped his father trap them, dropping stones down the centre of a stack while Eamonn the Miner waited at the only exit not barricaded with sods and clay, a broken graip handle for a club. To his son's admiration the system seldom failed. The Miner a systematic man: more method than madness here, unlike the grand-da.

'If you could meet all things middling,' his father held—until one day hearing his own advice he gave up on the mountain. It happened around the time he bought the ruins of Maguire's byre, using the stone to enlarge his own cowshed with the help of his two sons. Having paid good money for ready rock, Eamonn the Miner seldom spoke of gold again.

There had not been a cow in the byre for some years, the machine-cut Bord na Mona turf under its roof, the frost a threat to nothing more than Colum's bones. When Michael moved in after Dinny's mother died, the two brothers built a stack each autumn from the lorry load of turf dumped beside the lane. Taking turns on the short ladder propped against an end, they handed each other the clods for weeks, securing the stack with an old herring net that Michael kept in patient repair until his death. Now Denis Michael forked the entire load into the byre between dinner hour and tea of a single day.

Maybe it wanted a Californian after all. Setting down the bucket, Colum fumbled at his trousers, steam rising like the tea it once was. From the lane he heard his grandfather's voice come ghosting into the byre. 'I'm a miner, 49er, oh my darling, Clementine,' Colum sang along, the thin stream moving down the slurry trough to darken turf mould and old straw.

It took Denis Michael three days to land him, Colum knowing there was that much time or line, having heard the Yank had paid Nora McGinty a week's Bed & Breakfast in advance.

'You should see the size of him,' Francy Gara told Colum. 'In great big wellingtons from Maxwell's shop.'

'You could rent one and live in the other,' someone else observed of the footgear.

'An odd man, that. Like two left shoes,' said McGinty whose wife fixed the American rasher and eggs each morning.

'It's a golden opportunity,' Denis Michael told him when Colum at last agreed to see the visitor.

'It's myself has the gold, not he,' Colum saw his nephew to the door. Above the mountain a half moon shaped like a bowl lay tilted on end, spilling its light across the glen. 'I'm bound for California with a banjo on my knee,' Colum croaked, echoing Andrew Boyle to the great-grandson disappearing down the lane.

Francy Gara called by the morning of the visit, took in the Madeira loaf, packaged sweets, pound of butter in a single glance. Or perhaps it was the scoured oilcloth first caught his eye, its bemused expression like that on a small boy who, wandering into the kitchen, has his face suddenly scrubbed.

'Home was never like this,' Francy commented, taking more care than customary to hit the bucket of ash as he spat.

'Throw a sprat to catch a salmon,' Colum replied as he fed turf into the range.

'Will you sell then?' Francy fished, hoping for something he might peddle in the pub.

'I will not,' Colum said. 'It's only to have a proper tea.'

'If we do the thing, 'twill be well done,' he added by way of ending all discussion.

For all his great size Fred ate little of the spread the old man had provided. Easily six foot five, his head the entire time menaced the Sacred Heart hung above the sole armchair in the kitchen, threatening to dislodge the picture at any moment. He was a queer sort of specimen, agreed Colum with those in the pub, a pony tail as long as two summer days falling down his back. About Denis Michael's age he guessed, give or take a year.

The visit began with small talk. The Yank trying to fill with short sentences the longer moments of silence, the old man's contribution largely the hiss of spittle which he shook from his pipe onto the range. Nonetheless, it ended over an hour later midst bursts of animated conversation on the part of the visitor.

It was this talk that had let Colum down.

'He was on about some place in Scotland,' he told Dinny later that afternoon. 'Some community where they grow massive cabbages and the like. By talking to them he tells me!'

Outsized vegetables. Roses blooming in the snow. And a phenomenon called 'ley lines' which Colum did not pretend to understand.

' "You have them here!" he tells me. "Between the Church and the ruins of the court cairn." As if any eejit couldn't draw a straight line between two points.'

It was worse than a cruel trick—more like utter betrayal to have been sent a Yank like that. Believing in rubbish that suited Connie Meehan far more than any envoy from a land of technology and dreams. 'Sure America is on hard times,' they had told him in the pub. Well they might be, were his man Fred any indication of the new breed.

'It's worldwide, that,' had been Denis Michael's comment upon hearing of the magic cabbage. If he meant not ignorance but something else, a need for something beyond sight, taste and touch, something like gold, well, then he spared his uncle.

'Did you mention a price at all?' he asked after a time.

Colum said nothing for a while, his expression that of someone searching with his tongue for a piece of grit tasted in a mouthful of food.

'We did, but I won't sell,' he said at last. 'A big string of misery like that for a neighbour,' he shook his head. Seeing it was no weather for fishing, Denis Michael departed shortly. Fred was in Glenmore a few days yet. There was time enough.

It was as well he left, for Colum was in no mood. What odds whether he finished up with slates or thatch overhead; it would be sods above soon enough. Spying the bag of sweets, he took one out, unwrapped its wrapper. Stepping outside, he took in the ditches which marched across the far meadow to the deposit of gravel where streambed met the mountain. As if prompted by what he saw, he thought for a moment of the old fable, wondering would it have mattered any had all that the King touched turned to stone instead.

Taking another Brandy Drop from his pocket, he thought of his father who always took a last sweet with him along to bed. Something to suck on until sleep came. When Father Enright arrived with the Last Rites the morning the Miner died, Colum half expected the priest to remove a wafer-thin lozenge before administering the Host. To die without a sour taste in your mouth was perhaps something. To meet all things middling was not to strand yourself halfway between. To find yourself becalmed since summer off Byzantium. Looking up he was just in time to see a lump of blackbirds swirl across the meadow, to blow like smoke into the mountain face.

Nettle Broth

They were in the small crafts-shop next to the Church when its eye caught Cassie's own. It looked like a fish-eye, of coloured glass, mounted simply on a silver band. She called the other girls over but none of them seemed to fancy the ring; her sister Beryl said that it gave her the chills. The woman in the shop, noticing their interest, told them the jeweller lived on the mountain, a local man of twenty-five or so who shared a cottage with several other lads. Of a sudden the others began to admire bracelets and pendants surrounding the ring which Cassie half-expected to blink from the light shining into the display case. As they left the shop, they talked of calling on the mountain in a day or so.

There were four of them in it, on a holiday in a rented chalet on the coast of Donegal. The chalet of the advertisement turned out to be nothing fancier than four block walls partitioned within by chipboard into two bedrooms and a combined dining and sitting room. The bedroom walls stopped a foot short of the ceiling but nobody minded, for the weather had held since their arrival and there was little need of sitting around the place. Cassie was delighted to be away. Even if it poured day and night, she told herself, she was well rid of Dublin. Home of late had been more of a hell than usual, with himself drunk for most of the last month. 'Our father's a bit of a fugher,' Beryl had told the other girls the night before, causing Cassie to wonder at her own lack of any response to such a statement beyond a touch of envy at her sister's frankness. Since there had been nobody at the department store with whom she cared to share a holiday, both of the other girls were friends of Beryl from the Bank.

They found the jeweller's cottage the next morning, taking an unpaved lane which branched up the mountain from the main road along the coast. The other lads were away at work in the weaving mart, but the jeweller invited them into a converted out-building which served him as a workshop. The first thing Cassie remarked were the eyes which glanced about him with a gaze much like that of the rings he fashioned. Looking closer, she saw it was the amount of iris which showed beneath the pupil, giving him a wide-eyed look like the black-faced sheep they'd passed coming up the mountain. He was small, wiry to the extent that called actual wire to mind in the way he moved his arms with their suggestion of strength, his hair flying out from his head. Her sister said later she thought him a wee bit mad, all those words about rock and stone, explaining that the mountain above and the strand below were identical but for their scale, that the same quartz which composed the cliffs formed the sand by the sea as well.

He spoke continuously but softly—full of odd words—describing how some gems were formed by fusion, the girls exchanging a secret smile as he praised the quality of cleavage in other precious stones which allowed them to split in certain regular directions, yielding smooth plane surfaces. In answer to her question, he said the glass eyes of the rings came from an outfit in America which supplied the taxidermy trade, showing Cassie a colour catalogue with pages of eyes peering out—something for every fish, fowl, or beast to be stuffed.

Whereas some stones reflect light, he explained, the ruby absorbs, drinking in every colour but those which cause the sensation of red. 'The red of the ruby is that of pigeon blood, the blood of a dove.'

'Have you any rubies or diamonds about?' one of Beryl's friends asked with a laugh.

'I haven't,' he answered, then showed them a stone set in a ring. 'It's not my own work; the ring belonged to my grandmother. As I have no sisters, my mother gave it to me.'

'What stone is that?'

'Alexandrite.' He turned on the lamp over the work bench, and they watched as its grass-green shade turned a colour between pink and red under the fluorescent light. 'I used to play with it for hours as a child.'

Putting down the ring he took a piece of what looked like purple glass from a small box on the shelf.

'Amethyst . . . it's quartz as well, the same as these hills and strand. You can find fragments below where the river meets the sea. The name comes from the Greek—"without drunkenness": the ancients used to make their goblets from the stone, thinking it would keep them sober.'

'Perhaps we can commission such a glass for father,' Cassie heard Beryl whisper behind her as they peered around the shed with its disarray of metal scrap, crucibles, pliers, hacksaw blades, and burners. At the edge of the work bench hung a metal tray suspended by small chains. The bottom of the tray was perforated with small holes like a colander through which the silver dust trapped by the tray fell into a small tobacco tin attached to its underside. Looking closer, Cassie saw the dust filed off a set of rings still on the bench lying scattered across the tray—like silver salt or sugar spilt on a kitchen table.

'You might find some amethyst, yourselves, along the stream-bed,' Declan told them as they said goodbye. Yet that evening when she left the others all Cassie saw along the bank was the silver flash of tiny trout startled by her shadow.

It was June when they left, July when she came back. Her return to Donegal might well have been more a flight from father and home than an act of faith in Declan, had it not been for their last outing before the holiday was up. It was not their first time together, though, for Cassie had met Declan along the road the day after their visit to the workshop. It was not entirely coincidence since she had set off in that direction, leaving the rest to chance and luck. They'd walked the strand together looking for driftwood, and one night he and the two weavers had taken the four girls up to the lounge of the local hotel which opened from June to September. One of the weavers had got fairly drunk while

Declan scarcely touched his glass.

The day before they left, however, he and Cassie thumbed fifteen miles through a mountain pass to another stretch of coast where the edge of a vast strand ended against a towering cliff with a string of caves hollowed out of its belly. The largest cave had a massive entrance, its mouth worn into a series of arches like the stonework above cathedral doors that Cassie had seen once in a book on France. Standing there, they tried catching in their mouths the tiny drops of water which fell from a plant growing out of the rock where the keystone might have fitted.

They followed the cave back into its night, leaving their shoes by the door, rolling their trousers to the knee when they came to tidal pools along the floor. The walls were wet and cold to the touch, but adjusting to the dark, they were soon able to move without holding on. Wearing above her waist only the top of her swim-suit, Cassie could feel the cold air as it bathed her back and shoulders. They held hands for the last ten yards or so, and as they stood listening in the darkness to the slap of the incoming tide, Cassie sensed within herself some murmured response to the sea and the man beside her. As Declan was worried they might be trapped by the filling tide, they did not linger—yet from that moment Cassie fancied that should she return to Donegal, it would be a journey forward.

She came back a month later, shortly after a letter from Declan with word that the other two in the cottage, having been sacked from the weaving mart, had departed the village. It had been seldom ever easy with them in the cottage: the larger man was greatly given to drink, and came winding home most winter nights through the mist and damp in a leather German greatcoat with its brown fur collar and a bullet hole through the chest. Once after locking the door by mistake Declan and the other lad wakened to a tremendous crash. Next morning they found their companion curled asleep on the kitchen floor amid great drunken snores and tiny shards of glass. Finding himself without a key he had pulled the greatcoat over his head and dived through the kitchen window. He and his weaving-mate shared the other bedroom where on his worst nights he would tie up the smaller lad and paint wild murals on the wall.

It was in that bedroom that Cassie slept for the first fortnight. Though she'd given a week's notice at the department store, the only notice she gave at home was a note on her sister's pillow. The day she came they walked up far behind the cottage to a bog lake beneath the mountain's ridge. The heather was coming on and there were bees at the early flowers as they walked through waist-high ferns. Below them lay irregular ditches which shaped the small fields like necklaces of stone flung down at an evening's end. Continuing to climb they came upon a small hole in the grass on the hill. Looking in they saw water flowing, but strangest was the sound it made, echoing in the hollow darkness as it rushed beneath the mountain. And as she lay there beside him the first night they shared a bed, it was to that same sound she listened—beneath the whisper of his breathing. He was as virgin as she, but somehow they managed, shivering beneath the blanket despite the warm summer night. And if it had been his language that first attracted her, she soon came to feel the very words themselves, to feel herself all filigree and arabesque beneath his touch.

There was often an extravagance about his musings, that buried in the bog he hoped the weight of the sod might slowly over the years compress his body until all that remained would be a single emerald. Yet he wasn't obsessed with stones and rare metal, maddened by precious gems. Silver was only extracted after it was combined with lead he often remarked, and it was always better to keep your head about you. The graphite in a pencil was the same carbon as a diamond, only the structure of their crystals differed ... a definite triumph for form over content.

Indeed he was all bits and bobs of information, telling her that the emery board she used on her nails was made from powdered corundum, the very stone of rubies and sapphires. There were none among those she'd known in Dublin like him, nor was there much chance of meeting one among the louts who might kick your shin as an invitation to dance, some of them finding it enough of a struggle to remain standing with their great swollen faces red with drink. Beryl had introduced her to several boys from the Bank but they had all seemed quite dull, with none of the talk of this lad from Donegal who told her tons of tin were used annually to put the sheen and rustle into a pair of women's stockings. She had little need for stockings now, and began to let the hair on her legs grow, finding it too much a bother to heat water in a kettle simply to shave her legs.

It remained dry through August, the warmest summer in memory. The fine weather brought a great number of visitors so that Declan was busy filling orders for the crafts-shop and several merchants who sold his work along with curios carved from peat and coloured postcards. Happy as she was, Cassie was often lonely. She sensed a considerable reserve on the part of the few neighbour women with whom she seldom spoke, but when she mentioned it to Declan he said that it was their natural way. 'Ach, they're so cautious they scarcely speak to one another.' He himself came from the northern end of the county, had moved to this stretch of its southwestern coast two years before.

The few chores around the cottage that took up the morning were anything but tedious: indeed there was a novelty to much of her surroundings that often captivated. Life in the country contrasted with Dublin not only on a scale as grand as the mountains and sea outside their door, but in small details as well, like the white and gold-green flecks of chicken shit on the eggs, or the boggy taste of water from the tap instead of chlorine. Once more in the country, Cassie found herself recalling moments long since forgotten of a childhood's summer on her grandparents' farm in Tipperary. On cooler evenings when Declan lit a small fire she would remember her grandfather remarking how healthy turf smoke was, full of buried herbs, far better for you than the coal her family burned in Dublin—covering you with soot if you so much as looked at it. Memory did not always so directly erase the years between: at times triggered more by metamorphosis so that their fireside set of poker, tongs, shovel and brush brought back to Cassie her grandfather's pipe knife, a curious cluster of tiny tools which had enthralled her for evenings at a time.

She spent hours now among the hills, sometimes bringing back wild flowers for the kitchen. Bluebells had dominated during the holiday with the girls, entire fields of flowers seeming to float above the grass like a suspension of blue oil on a sea of green. By August ragwort had captured the pastures, its yellow everywhere. On hot afternoons the cows she passed breathed with a sound like bellows moving the heavy air. Still Cassie sensed it was a place more wild than pastoral, experiencing sometimes a strange reversal of mood in the landscape which she walked, as the afternoon she found a lamb washed up on the small strand below the road which only the day before had seemed the most gentle and intimate of places. Occasionally a gust of wind blew up whose force belied the summer air, driving the shirts hung crucified to flail wildly on the line.

One night after a gale woke them, they lay there listening to the wind whip round the cottage like a giant blanket shaken out, the rain striking the windowpane with a sound like sand. Rising once in the middle of the night Cassie saw an unearthly glimmer—like moonlight on the floor. Looking closer she saw it came from a glass dish in which they had set a fish to salt, its flesh now giving off a ghostly luminescence, glowing like the precious stones of which her lover spoke.

Donegal brought a change in her diet as well. Although she arrived late in the sowing season, she sent to a Dublin seed-store so that within a month they had a small patch with cress, carrots, and tiny radishes growing. At home it was always meat. For years when her father's shop had done poorly, it had been mostly offal: head, heart, and tongue, tripe made into a soup with milk, streaky rashers, black-pudding, liver or kidneys frying in the kitchen with a smell like someone had peed in the corner. After her uncle landed a job with a meat wholesaler her father was able to buy for the shop at a lower cost and the business improved somewhat.

They had a roast every Sunday then, but Cassie was never one for the meat. Years ago her mother had served up a jelly made from a mould in the shape of a rabbit. The jelly had quivered on the plate before them and Cassie, who was no more than four, thought the rabbit was alive. It put her off meat for several years, a situation which provoked her father no end during countless meals.

He berated Cassie most when he was drunk, and she found that her most vivid memories as a child had him always in his bloodied apron, his large red hands flecked with white like a pound of mince. He was not an attractive man, middling tall and heavy, more bloated now from drink than beefy. The rims of his lower eyelids, red and swollen, protruded like a bully's sullen nether lip.

Declan seldom ate meat and now so did she. Sometimes he killed fish for their dinner at the rocks below. The crabs which crawled into the lobster creels were of no use to the fishermen who would give Declan a half dozen of the large claws which Cassie baked on tongs laid over the fireplace embers. Among the used books in the chemist shop she found a volume on wild flowers containing recipes for sorrel soup and nettle broth. She tried the sorrel soup at once but hesitated at the nettles, not believing that anything so hateful could be eaten.

That summer in Tipperary she had reached unwittingly into a clump of nettles, her hands to sting for hours until her grandfather came home. Taking her into the garden he pulled another weed from the ground. 'Dockins, dockins, cure a nettle,' he chanted, slapping its leaves against her hands. 'Sure that is why you'll always find dockin and nettle growing side by side,' he told her.

The sting eased, but that night she dreamt the back of her hands were covered with small red lumps. Squeezing one, she saw a wee green shoot pop up. When she pulled the sprout it came free, bringing a clump of her hand with it like the earth around small roots. Wakening, she lay there weeping until her grand-da came in to comfort her again.

Now finding a pair of old gloves, Cassie carefully cut the tops off young nettle plants and made a broth, thickening it with milk and oatmeal. The milk she got from the old couple who rented Declan the cottage. Theirs was the highest dwelling on the mountain, a hundred yards further up the lane which passed by the younger couple's door. After the old woman gave Declan a pint of milk when he came once with the rent, Cassie began to climb the hill each morning with an empty bottle. Although she spoke so rapidly through her few remaining teeth that Cassie did not always understand, the old woman had none of the reserve of the other neighbours. Indeed the first morning that Cassie appeared, the old woman hoisted her skirts to show how swollen were her knees with the arthritis that no longer allowed her to milk and made churning a particular chore. Her husband rose early to milk, then returned to bed. Soon Cassie began to call afternoons as well.

'Are you not better off on the mountain,' she told Cassie, 'than to be on the road where you could live or die with nothing ever to happen. All that traffic, but nobody stops, nobody comes to call. Besides, from this height we can scatter ashes on every neighbour in the townland!' Leaning over in her chair she laughed herself upright, flinging her palms up to the ceiling, ballasted below by a pair of her husband's outsized shoes.

If there seemed little enough happening on the mountain either, it never occurred to Cassie to say as much. Rather she sensed a contentment on the part of the old woman surprisingly like that she had come to find with Declan and Donegal, and she found herself increasingly drawn to Maggie Ann, as the older woman was called. 'Refuse nothing, only the blows!' she once told Cassie, insisting that the younger woman accept a gift of buttermilk. She was utterly generous, offering onions and turnip from her garden, and Cassie began to set aside an occasional fish from Declan's catch.

Maggie Ann was generous in other ways also, never making the sly enquiries that Cassie half expected from the start. Instead, accepting Cassie and Declan as they were, she astonished Cassie on occasion. One morning after placing the plate of crabtoes on the table, she turned to Cassie with a wink.

'Aye should your man have a wild feed on those,

there'll be no sleep in it for you, my darling!' she laughed, throwing her hands up to the sky.

'Are they for that?' Cassie managed in a startled voice, thinking that it was more like talking to Beryl than with a woman the age of her grandmother.

'Faith, you don't think, now, that it's the lobster they go out after?' Maggie answered.

She taught Cassie to identify edible mushrooms, to check underneath where the stem joined the cap for worm holes. 'Sure there's no point washing them as they're the cleanest things there are.' She told Cassie that when she and her husband were courting, they would go up to the bog lake where Maggie roasted the wee trout he caught on a small stone set in the coals of a fire, mushrooms from the mountainside cooking in the juice of the trout.

'We used a stone instead of a pan, for once you brought a pan, you'd fancy a taste of salt, and once you had salt, 'twould only be something else.'

When Cassie mentioned the broth of nettles, Maggie Ann said it had been the favourite potage of the saint named for a dove, who centuries before lived in those very mountains.

'It was all he ate, with perhaps a taste of salt on Sunday . . . the people here would find the lines of his ribs in the sand where he had lain on the strand the night before.'

Somehow the story of the saint brought Maggie to Father Cunningham, the village priest, though she had small use for him. 'You couldn't find the ribs on him with your hands pressed flat against his chest . . . nor would I be dying for the chance to, either. And him with a great temper to match his bulk!'

'A rabid fox will feed on the lambs, soon as he's grown too weak for his natural prey,' her husband's only comment on the subject. Bringing the conversation back to the saint, he told Cassie how the holy man had driven demons into the sea below their cottage.

Cassie passed the priest once on the road, a man as large as her father, and the encounter frightened her. Mentioning it to Declan, she heard him say that he too had met the priest that day while coming up from the sea.

'I offered him a fish but he said he had no taste for it. And that was all he said. Last spring he asked did I do any metalwork, something about a pair of candlesticks for the side-altar, but I've heard nothing since.'

'Perhaps I'll have to make an honest woman of you, Cass, to get my commission back,' he added after a pause.

'You can go to hell!' she told him quickly. Yet if angered by his humour, it soon passed.

'Sure we've scarcely known one another long enough to be talking of a thing like marriage.'

They'd both laughed at that, but in bed that night she lay remembering what the nuns had said of sin. That a venial sin might tarnish the soul, but never blacken it as mortal sin does. Black as coal, black as her soul. Black was the absence of all colour, Declan said, a truly black stone absorbs the entire spectrum, drinks in the rainbow. White was all colours, the colour of God's angels. The nearer the Church, the farther from God, according to Maggie Ann. The farther from God, the father from God. God the Father save us from our fathers she thought, and fell asleep.

When Declan worked at night in the old turf shed, Cassie read by the fireside, a habit more of her childhood than recent years, though it had been scarcely easy even then with a school that never allowed books home, and her mother who thought library books were covered with other people's germs and so 'a dirty risk'. Purchasing some odd ends of wool at the weaving mart, Cassie also began to knit, another endeavour that she'd set aside some years before. Yet it gave little satisfaction: she seemed always in a hurry—until one night when she remembered the reason for the rush. On the farm that summer her grandfather had told a story of a girl whose seven brothers were turned into swans. Although many in the village put it down to some evil the sister had done, an old woman whispered to the girl that by knitting them each a coat of nettles before sunrise, she could save her seven brothers. Quickly gathering the nettles, the girl knitted all night, blood dripping from her fingers. As dawn broke and the villagers came for her, she had knitted all but a sleeve of the seventh coat. As her brothers flew over, she flung the coats into the air. The brothers recovered their human form, all except the youngest who in place of an arm had a long white wing. Waiting until Declan would leave the cottage, Cassie began a jumper for him, hoping to have it done by Christmas.

Although there was no great selection of books at the chemist shop, Cassie brought back a battered dictionary with half of its red jacket missing. Looking up the language her jeweller lover used, she smiled to think of blushing at a dictionary, yet marvelled at how sexual much of their meaning seemed. What she had first sensed along her body with 'arabesque'—*a fantastic ornament among Spanish Moors consisting of plant, foliage and vine curiously intertwined*—she now saw confirmed in small printed type. Foliage and vine wound through their converse also, as she read aloud to Declan from the book of wild flowers. Winding bindweed and primrose into his talk of stones, she was reminded of a childhood game: 'Are you Animal, Vegetable, or Mineral?' Beryl would ask as they lay in bed. If death turned Declan to an emerald, perhaps she might become a plant? Indeed she felt as if already she had set down fine tiny roots like silver hairs, there in Donegal.

One night Declan spoke, bringing her halfway back from wherever it is that you go asleep.

'Could you ever guess how few ounces of platinum would make a wire from Dublin to New York City?'

'Go to sleep.'

'You would need but seven.'

'It wouldn't be far enough from Dublin to please me,' she murmured back. Yet in a certain sense she had come further than Donegal since leaving home. Always curious, her curiosity now seemed to know no bounds. Much of it came from Declan's talk, explaining that turquoise took its name from Turkey, or why the Plaster was of Paris. Or agate named for a river in Greece. But Declan in turn listened and learned when she read aloud at night, and Cassie began to look for books on history at the chemist's.

Still the dictionary fascinated her most, as if she read something of herself and certain moments of her life with Declan in words like 'temper' and 'anneal' with their description of *glass and metals strengthened by subjection to great heat and gradual cooling*. She wondered at the paradox of something steeled through its very softening, but guessed at a similar change within herself over the past months. That day at the caves she had swum in the filling tide, delighted by the strange weaving motion of the sea-wrack underwater. Declan had not done so, and for the first time Cassie considered that in some ways she might be stronger than he. On the road back they caught a ride in a vegetable van, sitting midst crates of onions from New Zealand, Israeli oranges, bananas from Panama. Yet if on that day she apprehended her own mettle, it had been only in opposition to him, whereas now it seemed a thing of her very own.

Filigree with its *convoluted forms in silver and gold* itself recalled an early discussion with Declan. She had expressed a preference for gold, he for silver. After informing her that gold was extracted in a cyanide bath with arsenic as a by-product, he stopped laughing and grew silent for a time.

'You know, Cass, if gold is truly king of metals and silver queen, then I'm as wrong in my preference as you in yours . . . And didn't you play with your grandfather's knife, and I with my grandmother's jewels?'

Looking back now she felt that he had said something there, only there was nothing wrong with it at all, and she wondered if she loved him for his silver gentleness much as he left her her new found fibres of gold.

Months passed and October came. After tea Cassie gathered brambleberries until in the gathering darkness she could no longer see the berries which seemed to melt into the shadow between leaf and vine. A week later the berries were gone, those yet on the bushes overripe now with a fermented taste like the memory of wine. The air had turned colder, the ferns on the mountain turned iron red as if the stone beneath had rusted through. Crows flew above the harvested cornfields, the edges of their wings sharp against the evening chill. One night when Declan called her outside, she saw on the water below red, gold and green lights of the herring boats, rising and falling on the swell like the candles of some holy procession. Through the dark came the muted mutter of engines, running softly over the sound of the sea.

'Who are you writing?' Declan asked one evening.
'My sister Beryl.'
'Beryl, the mineral, can be both emerald and aquamarine. It's also the magic stone used in the fortune teller's crystal ball, I believe.'
'Ummmh,' said Cassie lost in the letter.
'It would be handy to have an article like that here, wouldn't it? Let you know what to expect each morning? Weather forecast and all.'
'I can live without one,' Cassie said, lifting her head from the table. In fact she had never felt so much at peace with the future, giving it little thought past plans for the grand garden she would put in next spring.

There are more ways to read the future than

magic stones alone, however, and one sunny morning Cassie rose to find the raindrops in the fuchsia shining like bits of shattered glass. That evening as she stood at the sink preparing the tea she heard a slap on the floor behind her. Turning she saw the headless gutted fish that Declan had left on the table, flipping and slapping its body against the tile. Later, in the pot where she had boiled its head and tail for stock, she saw the fish eyes turned small and white like the wee mothballs in her mother's wardrobe. From their bed that night she heard the Church bell in the village strike the hour, a sound more flat than hollow, like someone beating on an old scrap of iron.

Perhaps she even recognized the sound of her father's fist on the door at dawn, before she heard him bellow. Rising from the bed, she half drew a robe around her so that the morning light as she opened the door half fell upon her breast.

'Have ye no respect for the Father!' the butcher shouted as she glimpsed the figure in black behind him.

'Get stuffed, you drunken bastard,' she answered softly in a voice barely raised at all.

He lifted his hand but she got there first, a fine hard slap across his face until his own hand sent her stumbling into Declan's arms. She tried to hold Declan back but he tore away and rushed her father with a curse. The blow from the butcher lifted the jeweller into the air and against the wall where they all heard the sound of the bone give: a dry snap like driftwood breaking. Though Declan kept his feet, his arm now hung at his side like a crippled wing. By then the priest was between them and her father, the butcher threatening to make mincemeat of the smaller man whose face was as white as milk.

'Come, my daughter,' said the priest, holding out a hand.

'You'll not find Glasgow like life in Donegal, Declan or no Declan,' Beryl told her at home. All the same she gave Cassie money for the passage and a new dress. The crossing was rough, the sea up, and Cassie ate only a watery cup of packaged soup. 'Ox-tail,' the boy behind the counter told her. Too tired and tensed to read, she sat at the table looking down at her hands, the stone on her finger changing colour as the lights overhead pitched with every roll of the boat.

In the village the story went that she'd left Dublin again, only this time for New York City with a married man. Maggie Ann who heard the talk before she died laughed in the face of the neighbour who told her so. Father Cunningham remained in the village, of course, continuing to play the shepherd to his flock, having an occasional leg of lamb of a Sunday, and keeping a sharp eye out for the wandering sheep.

Fables

His mother showed Michael the letter after pouring him the cup of tea he always took upon his return from school. It was a typewritten note from the County Hospital, stating that a Heaf Test administered to Michael McNelish at the Glenmalin National School registered a positive reaction. His mother was advised to contact the hospital to arrange for a chest X-ray as soon as possible. Until she read of the X-ray his mother had wondered if Heaf should not have been Deaf. His grandfather Paddy said Heaf was an English word for sheep pasture, but then Uncle Dinny who had travelled to America dropped by, to explain that Heaf was a test for tuberculosis, and a chest X-ray would reveal any spots upon the lungs.

Michael stared at his name which he had never before seen in tiny black print. Recalling the bubble injected under the skin of his forearm a fortnight before—to turn into a red blister—he began to consider the possible spots on his lungs. Yet all that came to mind was something like the dirt on a freshly washed jumper for which his mother sometimes scolded him when she was angry with his father.

'I tell you heaf has to do with pasturage in England,' insisted his grandfather from his customary chair beside the range. In the colder months he wore as many as three vests, two waistcoats, and a jumper, all of them beneath his tattered jacket. Embers from his pipe had pocked his apparel so thoroughly that Michael's mother declared his clothes were like a sieve, and that he needed at least five layers to save his skin.

'And how many sheep did you ever see grazing in London?' she now tossed back at him.

'I worked on the underground for a week only,' her father replied. 'And it would break your heart to see the work I did. In water up to your neck, shovelling out clay seven days a week. Digging your own grave it was. You couldn't stick it for long, not unless you were one of those great big Connemara lads, six feet tall and wide as a door, able to live on drink and a crust of bread.' Although Paddy spoke often of Connemara, he had in his life spent no more than six months outside Donegal, to see far more of London and Glasgow than ever he would of Galway, county or town.

Uncle Dinny advised that Michael no longer milk, should he indeed be infected. His father muttered that the lad did little enough as it was, but his mother accepted her brother's advice. To Michael the news that he would escape a chore suddenly suggested the seriousness of his condition, even more than the official-looking letter had done. Once again he turned to the problem of the spots, wondering were they anything like those that appeared on your face. As he finished his tea he heard his grandfather remark that goat's milk was once held to be good against tuberculosis.

Still, it wasn't a cure like donkey's milk for the whooping cough that Michael as an infant had contracted. His father and Paddy setting out on a moon-flooded night for the mountain where John Byrne's donkey was nursing a foal: his father to tie the jenny's legs while Paddy filled a jam jar. Paddy to handle the descent from the mountain that night as easily as his son-in-law, despite some forty years difference in age. But stiffness overtook him soon thereafter, and for a long time Michael wondered where it was that this Arthur Itis who so plagued his grand-da lived.

Even now it seemed to Michael that words often hindered as much as they helped. If the master sometimes spoke of a negative attitude toward his lessons, a positive reaction to a test now indicated that he might be ill. And his friend Packy Gara, a year ahead at school, claimed positive and negative applied to numbers also.

'Why if it were TB he had, you'd see two bright spots of red on his cheeks, as they used to sing of Nellie in the song. I mind well the family of five daughters, neighbours they were, and every one of them stricken with it.' Pausing, his grandfather took a reddened wire from the range, using it to ream a length of reed that would replace a broken pipe stem. 'Sure it's all cancer these days, no word of TB at all.'

'Of course there's nothing on him,' his mother said with a sharp look at the old man. 'Go out and get the turf,' she added, turning back to Michael.

Even without the milking there would be work enough, thought Michael as he headed for the turf shed. Besides, the cow within six weeks of calving gave little milk as it was. Yesterday evening, huddled against her swollen flank for warmth in the November chill, she had caught him flush across the cheek with a great plashy swipe of her mucky tail. In return he cracked her across the neck, though not severely, for fear that she would stop giving milk altogether. Once after she tossed a tramcock two mornings in succession, his father beat her so harshly that she gave him nothing for his tea for months, responding to Michael's mother's touch alone.

Although his grandfather's talk had provoked his mother, it was the old man himself who bore a scar beneath his lip from a cancer operation. Treatment with needles at the County Hospital having failed, they sent him to Dublin where he stayed for eleven nights, playing cards at all hours in the ward with men from every county. 'You can't beat a Donegal man,' the head nurse told him after the operation, sending up a hot punch to his bed that evening. The doctor told him to give up smoking, but Paddy refused at first. Until one night on his return from the pub when he threw an unopened package of Woodbines onto the strand below the road. There was nothing in the way of weather that night, and next morning Paddy went down early to search for the cigarettes along the strand.

Once when he was Michael's age, helping with the hay on the north side of the glen, young Paddy had been asked by an old man with drink taken to do the job of lighting his pipe. The old man had been also too drunk to mince the tobacco properly, and Paddy had to pull and pull on the pipe. It made him sick to his stomach, so sick that he began to vomit under an August sun. He lay down behind a ditch to recover, yet later entering the house to sit by the range, he would be sick all over again.

Despite doctor's orders Paddy never kicked the pipe, but he went off cigarettes at last, all the time threatening to begin again, now that he couldn't make Lent on them anymore. His trip to the Dublin hospital had been ten years before, with himself nearly seventy and Michael a year old. Three years later his wife died and Paddy came to live with his daughter's family. All Michael remembered of the wake was his grandmother asleep in her bed as waxen as a candle. Now that his brothers were all in England, Michael shared the lower bedroom with his grandfather alone. If he ever thought of a room to himself, he was not oblivious of the fire that his mother laid in the grate for the old man during the winter months. Above the fireplace hung a likeness of Christ belonging to Paddy, its face entirely blackened by the small lamp of paraffin oil with its red glass globe resting on the shelf beneath.

To Michael his grandfather had been always the oldest person in the world. A child of two or three, he had delighted in the old man: indeed to hear his mother tell it, the two of them seemed to exist only to torture one another. Michael crawling all over his grandfather seated beside the range in his own kitchen then, while Paddy pulled the lad's cheeks until they were bright red, wreathing them both in the smoke from his pipe. Mingled with the smell of tobacco was the sweet rotting odour of apple peelings that Paddy carried in his jacket, a treat for his donkey who was nearly thirty years himself.

Yet if Michael's first memories embodied his grandfather, they were no match for the story Paddy told of his own father who lived to be ninety-six. One day the great-grandfather fell into conversation with a visitor from America who marvelled at the changes the aged man described in his lifetime.

'You must have a fine memory,' remarked the Yank. 'How far back can you recall?'

'The sound of the dog barking in the lane at the mid-wife as she made her way home ... I mind it as it were yesterday.' A man of remarkable health, the great-grandfather never saw a doctor until he was in his sixties. 'When I was ill, I was too ill for the Doctor,' he often observed. Then one harvest he cut his leg with the scythe. Three days after bathing the wound in paraffin oil, he rode down to the dispensary on a donkey.

In those early years Michael hung on the tales his grandfather told of the old woman who lived among the caves by the Silver Strand, five miles down the coast from their cottage. One evening bringing the cows home across the bluff, she saw the faeries dancing on the sand below. A mere child then, she climbed down to join them, though it was not until she accepted their food that they captured her for life.

His first year at school however, the older boys laughed and said his grandfather was only telling stories. 'Do you ever tell lies, grand-da?' Michael asked at home.

'Not a word of them,' Paddy replied. 'There's

something to all those stories.'

'Ach, he's only pretending,' they told him at school. After a year there his confusion concerning the stories faded, and Michael soon learned the words 'old-fashioned' which he could apply whenever the old man told an occasional tale.

'Once they become scholars, it's all football and the like,' his grandfather held, adding in recent years television to his list of complaints. 'There was once a time when you couldn't leave the house at night for fear of meeting a ghost or the Devil, but now it's the live ones you fear! Never a word of the Devil now . . . Who knows, perhaps he's dead?'

Yet in the week following the letter from the hospital, Michael found himself again thinking of those fables—as if there were some connection between them and his present situation. If the idea that he might actually die seemed as fantastic as the stories themselves, magic at least offered the option of believing or not, whereas death which held no such alternative was at the same time entirely beyond belief.

As to a possible illness, Michael was of mixed minds. Uncle Dinny joked that they would need send him to Arizona for a cure, bringing strange landscapes and Indians to mind. However the first volume of the encyclopaedia at school was missing, and this prospect remained vague. His father said it would be merely a matter of weekly shots at the dispensary, but even this novel routine had its attraction—aside from the needles. His mother rang the hospital from the Post Office, arranging an appointment for the coming Monday.

And only then did Michael remember the tunnel.

He was on the football pitch when the thought stopped him in mid-stride, a donkey braying into the setting sun from somewhere up the north side of the glen. 'Come on, Mike! That's not the Angelus you hear!' Packy Gara scolded beside him, chest heaving beneath his gold and green football shirt.

'Every time a donkey brays, another tinker's dead,' said Michael quoting the grandfather. It was his grandfather also who'd first told him of the tunnel. In the Protestant churchyard, covered with a wooden door fitting flush into the grass. According to Paddy, a man and his dog had climbed into it one night, the dog to turn up in the town of Kilrush, fifteen miles from their village, but the man never to be seen again. The tunnel itself was listed in a book at school, *Ancient Ruins of Ireland*, which if it brought no renown upon Glenmalin, lured the occasional visitor there. Built around the ninth century it was described as a *souterrain*. When Michael asked what the Irish meant, the master responded to half his query, informing him that the word was French.

Packy and Michael dropped over the wall, then remained on their knees for fear of being seen. If it was a mortal sin to enter a Protestant church, less reason to be found poking around its boneyard. Shadows of burial stones lay strewn in long rectangular patterns across the grass, as if night were already falling in scattered blocks of black. Beyond the wall a shout carried from the football pitch, seeming to heighten their sense of trespass.

Lifting the trapdoor at either end, they laid it gently on the grass as though it were made of china. The entrance was a round hole like a well, dropping nearly seven feet to the bottom. Michael went first, hanging from his hands as his feet sought purchase on the stones below. Passing beneath a lintel formed by a massive slab, they found themselves in an inner chamber where night had truly fallen. Feeling the damp air on his cheeks, Michael thought of his grandfather in the London underground. As if to reassert his seniority after having followed him below, Packy fumbled mightily for the matches that accompanied his cigarettes. He struck them one by one, and in the intermittent bursts of light they peered at the wet walls of stone which formed a room served by a second door smaller than that through which they'd entered.

'That way to Kilrush,' said Michael, making no move in its direction. With the last of the matches they discovered a stick-like object in a corner of the chamber, its colour the curious yellow of a bone never bleached by the sun.

'Chicken,' Packy said and Michael agreed. Ignoring the other passageway by mutual if unspoken consent, they climbed quickly up to the world above. Packy suggested catching a lift on the tractor taking trash to the dump where they could hunt rats with rocks, but Michael turned him down. There was milking to be done at home he said. On the road back he ignored the few blackberries yet on the vine. 'After Hallow's Eve the Devil spits on them and makes them his own.' If he didn't believe his grandfather, still he didn't want to pick up a disease or anything from them.

Sunday finally arrived. At Mass the entire congregation wheezed and coughed, groaning its way through the responses until it seemed to Michael that he was kneeling inside a giant lung. Each moment of silence troubled by a single cough somewhere in the pews which ignited another and so on, much as a single dog at night will set off all the others in a townland. A rooster crowing in the dark worked the same way. Yet his grandfather set great store by roosters, saying that he would sooner part with all his hens than lack a rooster around the cottage. 'A rooster keeps the Devil away.'

'Sure that's only talk,' his mother would reply, preferring to hear less mention of the Old Fellow about her kitchen.

'Oh, there's something in it,' insisted her father. 'For in the time of Christ, Our Lord, didn't they throw the dead cock into the pot, and didn't the cock get up on the rim and crow three times? St. Peter himself will tell you that,' he finished up.

During the sermon the priest admonished the parishioners to clean the graves in the churchyard. If a neighbouring grave had no one left to keep it tidy, then clean it also as an act of charity. At dinner his grandfather remarked that they saved hay from the graveyards in Connemara.

After tea Michael went down to the bottom of the pasture where the grass gave way to rocks that fell down to the water. It was late in the year for fishing, but the sea was down and there had been fowl above the water all afternoon. He called to the gulls as they swerved down over the waves, talking aloud to himself every time he cast too near the wrack where his line might foul. At first he thought the line indeed had snagged when the fish struck, stopping the reel dead. Lifting the rod high above his head, he swung a several-pound pollock onto the rock. Trapping it beneath his foot, he freed the hook from its gaping mouth. As he struck its head against the rock, blood splattered like thick red paint across the black toe of his wellingtons. The fish fell from his hands into a tidal pool on the rock, gliding onto its side so that its scales shone green through the water, something strange in its motion like the movement in a dream.

Facing the sea again, he saw the last of the sunlight catching the tower high on the mountain head across the bay. Last week the Master had called it a Martello Tower—yet if Michael had wondered what Martello meant, he hadn't asked the Master. His grandfather said the mortar for the tower was made from lime and oxen-blood. In fact Paddy was full of odd knowledge as well as the fantastic, able to announce the death of a lamb by the grey crows hovering above the pasture in the morning, warning Michael's mother to keep a sharp eye out for magpies until the baby chicks were old enough to fend for themselves.

After Mass that morning the old man and Michael's father had quarrelled over a seal that had poached on his father's salmon net that spring. His father waiting with a rifle from a ledge overhanging the sea where the net was buoyed, to miss with the only shot he got. Their argument was not over that seal so much, but concerned a neighbour who once killed fifty seal, collecting two hundred pounds in the bounty paid on their snouts in an attempt to protect the fishing.

'Not right, that, to slaughter seal so. Or foxes.'

'And it's right to let them tear into your nets, as that cheeky bastard did with me last May?' his father said angrily.

'If it were right, would your man have lost seventy sheep the following year? He has not hunted seal since, I believe.'

Seeing that his son-in-law had no answer there, Paddy went on to decry the fertiliser that ran off the fields with the rain, ran into the river once renowned for its trout. And the new nylon nets with their smaller mesh that the seiners now used.

'Great big nets which reach down to the bottom of the sea and scrape it clean, spawn and all. And so each year the catch is smaller. When you have lived as long as I, it's not hard to see what the problem is . . . Making things better to make things worse!'

'It's not old you are, but old-fashioned; that's a fact,' muttered his son-in-law upon departing the kitchen. An accusation that left Michael feeling as if he had betrayed his grandfather, as surely as if he had uttered the words himself.

As angry as his father grew at times with Paddy, he never lost his temper in the manner that he might with his own children. That summer the older lads had returned from England on their holidays. While they were making the haystack from the countless tramcocks, Sean, the youngest of the three, broke the handle of a rake. As their father stood cursing and fuming astride the stack, Sean and the others lowered their heads, only to grin sideways at one another. To Michael the idea that one might separate their father's temper from the man himself came entirely as a surprise. Although he often played an apostle of the modern to Paddy, his father took pride in the haying rakes which he fashioned by hand, whittling the teeth out of blackthorn. Sean said that the English made a liquor from the blackthorn fruit which they called sloe, though it was not spelled slow at all.

As if thought had the power to conjure, to call forth its images, Michael found himself staring at the largest seal he had ever seen. Its great grey head poking out of the sea not ten yards from where he stood, so near that he could see the lustre of wet fur along its neck. There had been a small seal on the strand below the road for several mornings of late on his way to school, but this seal was far larger, perhaps the very one grown fat on his father's salmon. Paddy said young seal on the strand were a sign of bad weather, a storm out to sea for them to be in so far.

While Michael stood motionless, the seal dove repeatedly: its body a brief shadow in the sea, then nothing. But each time it resurfaced, its black eyes fixing Michael with that strange expression somehow both empty and intense. Although he knew the seal by now had frightened off any fish, he waited on the rock—matching its curiosity with his own until it dove for the final time and he could no longer see its head, bobbing like the buoy on a lobster creel, anywhere on the water's surface.

That night the storm woke Michael from his sleep. The wind was from the north, sweeping past the tower on the bluff across the bay, and on his way to the toilet he heard the hailstones lashing against the kitchen door. He had wakened with a headache, making everything seem harsher as a result, as though even the furniture revealed by candlelight had taken on a rawer edge. Across the room the raggedness of his grand-da's breathing seemed to mock the gentle curve of his body beneath the bed-clothes, his own breath forming a cloud as it extinguished the candle flame.

By morning the wind had swung around to the east, leaving the sea still up from the night before. Several days of an east wind in winter brought frost, even to their end of the village that sat along the sea. Rising, Michael would see great white patches on the road, outsized imitations of the lichen which covered the stones in a ditch. There was no frost this morning, however, though the fuchsia beyond the kitchen door showed brown, sered by the hail that Michael alone had heard. Whatever he knew of the weather he had learned from his grandfather, who cautioned him that should the wind shift direction while he was making a face, he would wear that face forever. For a long time after Michael had never crossed his eyes outside the cottage.

His mother had arranged transport to Ballymurphy with Uncle Dinny who kept a Volkswagen purchased with his earnings from America. As they passed above the small strand, Michael saw no sign of young seal, or Woodbines, the sand as empty as the blackboard awaiting the young scholars at school, erased by the receding tide. Although he would escape class that day, any holiday feeling on Michael's part was more than tempered by the prospect of a hospital visit, painless as it was promised to be. Inside the Protestant churchyard a sheep leaned rubbing its neck against a gravestone.

Ballymurphy with its hospital lay thirty-five miles from Glenmalin, a little over an hour's drive.

Where the road turned from the coast they passed stands of pine that never failed to have their impact on Michael, for there were no trees in sight of the cottage, nothing beyond the bleached stump of an occasional bog oak on the mountain behind.

It was early yet when they pulled into Ballymurphy, the town still seemingly asleep, rainwater on sidewalk and street glistening as the sun broke through the clouds. There was little traffic, either foot or motor, most of the houses with waxed cartons of milk on window-ledges or beside their doors. A man in a white coat disappearing into a butcher's shop, a giant splayed pig across his shoulders.

Coming off the Diamond, they passed the castle that Michael's school had visited on an outing the previous year. It had been June, the trees surrounding the ruins filled with daws: flying from branch to branch and madly calling, until the trees themselves had seemed alive. The school bus had left the town that evening, the castle walls lit with spotlights that illuminated the site until the last visitors departed the county in late September. Over those same summer months ducks and swans swam in the river, below the green railroad bridge behind the castle. Though the birds returned each season, the train had disappeared long before Michael's birth.

They found the hospital, an old building behind an iron fence, its entrance hall stacked with unused furniture. Noticing a strong odour, Michael asked his mother who said it was something they used to keep the place clean. When asked if kept clean, why did it stink so, she told him to hush.

As they sat outside the X-ray room, two men in

white passed along the corridor, pushing a bed on wheels. They paused for a moment opposite, and Michael stared across at an old man who looked like Paddy. The same silver strand of hair across his brow, only the face was far more wasted. Both his eyes and mouth were open: yet he hardly seemed to see or breathe. Only his fingers moved, picking repeatedly at the bedsheet like a hen half-heartedly scratching outside the cottage door.

'Don't breathe!' the nurse cautioned him. Though he winced at the cold screen against his chest, it was over in a moment. 'You'll get a notice in the post in a fortnight or so,' she told his mother. 'And I'm sure it'll be negative!' she added cheeringly.

The letter took only a week to arrive, its news as good as she'd promised, but at the moment Michael was paying no mind to her at all. Even as he stripped off shirt and vest, the picture of the old man in the corridor had remained before his eyes, hanging there like some ghostly X-ray image all his own. He understood now that it was not to be himself—or tuberculosis either—that was involved this time, but rather Paddy. Suddenly he remembered his grandfather had yet to leave the bedroom that morning when Uncle Dinny arrived, and Michael had neglected to bid him goodbye.

'Finish your dinner, Michael,' his mother chided, pointing to the plate of chicken and chips lying practically untouched before him. Aware that he'd anticipated the meal out for an entire week, she guessed his preoccupation concerned the X-ray, and so held back from reminding him.

'It's too tough,' he complained, a response made possible only by his father's absence.

'Probably some rooster dead from old age,' Uncle Dinny said helpfully, having waited for them in the bar of a hotel on the Diamond. Telling Michael on the road back that his VW was for the Old Volks Home in another year or so.

On their way they passed through Kilrush where Michael failed to see a single dog, tunnel or not. Yet if he believed now, it was too much the death-bed conversion—even if it were not to be his own. He remembered the story Paddy told of a man who met a funeral procession one morning on the mountain road. When he inquired who had died, he heard his own name given back. To drop dead three days later on his way back from Mass. Though he feared what they might find at home, it seemed to Michael the road had doubled in length. Yet finally they were there.

Racing into the kitchen, he saw the chair beside the range empty. Touching the pipe lying there, he found it cold.

'Well, lad, you mended quickly!'

Turning, he saw his grandfather at the back door, the yellow milking pail at his side. Rushing to take the pail from him, Michael took the old man's hand instead, enclosing it within both his own. Three months later they buried Paddy, laying him underground on a frost-covered morning with the wind from the east, the sea as flat as a table.

Killing Time

The package lay on the table next to the butter dish. Below the postage its white wrapping had torn away, revealing the single word FLASH in red letters. A small rectangle, four inches long and an inch high, it was the kind of box which holds flashcubes for a camera. The address was correct:

> Dermot Doherty
> Glenmore
> Co Donegal.

Sent as registered mail with a return address, everything was in order—only Dermot knew nobody named Carr in Carrigaholt. And he had never owned a camera.

He had risen late with a terrible head, struggling out of bed only minutes before Hayes the postman appeared in the lane. Filling the kettle for tea, Dermot groaned aloud at the memory of Paddy Cannon the evening before. Small wonder that his head hurt so this morning.

Only after he finished the letter from the daughter in Arizona had Dermot given the parcel a second thought. If Glenmore was sixty miles from the border, still these were crazy times with the news full of letter bombs, and he suddenly grew suspicious. Dermot was not in the least political, but then neither was the small lad near Derry who bringing the cows home one afternoon the previous month walked over a land mine intended for the British Army. As Dermot's father often observed, with a war on it was far safer to be in uniform than not.

He lowered an ear to the parcel, then listened for half a minute; yet all he heard was a pounding in his head. Turning his attention to the kettle, he wondered would it ever boil. 'Must be a frog in it,' Maggie his wife would comment. No sooner had Dermot considered the possibility than he regretted it, feeling his stomach turn over on him as easily as a greased ball of dough in a mixing bowl.

But memory turned perverse (as it seemed to do increasingly of late) and ignoring the response from his stomach, Dermot recalled for the first time in years another morning long ago in Glenmore. The Dohertys had done as every family in the glen, drawing their water from a well or stream, until one year his father laid a line of second-hand pipe from a concrete tank that he fashioned on the mountainside above the cottage. At first to his father's pride and delight the water had flowed without a flaw into the kitchen; after a fortnight, though, the flow became a trickle until one morning to his mother's horror the elongated body of a frog slid slowly out the spigot itself.

Steam billowing from the kettle caught the sunlight coming through the window, catching his eye as well. He had eaten little for breakfast ever since

Maggie's death six months before, and this morning he was even less inclined toward eating. The hurt in his head felt like a crack several inches in width and still widening. The quality of pain reminded him of a painting job at the Navy Yard in Brooklyn his second year in the States. Having finished early that day, they began on the methyl alcohol supplied to thin the paint. An hour later Dermot felt as if it had thinned his blood instead as two companions carried him home.

Still you could probably strip the paint from a battleship with what he had drunk last night. Though not a steady drinker, he had gone down to McShane's pub for a quick pint as he might do once or twice a week. Paddy Cannon had been there with his mouth running like the sea in December, and Dermot was wishing he had stayed home when Andy Gillespie gave him an elbow in the ribs. Dermot followed him out to the toilet where Andy produced a bottle of poteen from under his jacket.

'I knew it wasn't another pub you were after coming from, Andy, when I saw you come in the door,' Dermot told him, raising the bottle to his mouth. McShane the publican knew what was up but seemed not to mind, and after a number of trips out back Andy and he had finished the bottle. By the time Dermot stumbled out the door, he was practically past hearing anything, Cannon or cannonfire included.

He'd met Maggie that same year of the painting job, in Brooklyn at a dance at the Hibernian Hall. Two years out of Ireland, Dermot was twenty-four years old. Two years later they married, moving to a flat in the Bronx where they began the family.

Three daughters and thirty-odd years later, they decided to return to Ireland. The daughters were all married and moved away, the house which they now owned seemed far too large, so they sold it and returned to Glenmore, choosing Dermot's Donegal over Maggie's native Cavan.

They moved into a small bungalow with central heating, yet with fireplaces for turf as well. Dermot suggested a range in the kitchen but Maggie had not been as eager. A year after they arrived she died. She left so suddenly that at times Dermot found himself regarding her death with something close to resentment, as if she'd taken a morning to go shopping without leaving him a note. The pain at first so acute had by now begun to dull, though on occasion he still felt the sudden shock of her absence, like looking up where a mirror usually hung to see not yourself but bare wall instead. His own health had worried them of late, concern for his high blood pressure, but it was Maggie who failed, suggesting to Dermot that whatever was lacking in the way of humour, the Lord had a steady sense of the ironic.

The problem now was that of an emptiness in his day. And night. Of late he had taken to reading in the evening; or when the tide was right he took a fishing rod across the meadow to the rocks below the cottage, as if he found there on the western coast of Donegal a loneliness to match his own.

The trick to killing time was not to injure yourself in the process, and for that reason alone Dermot knew drink was not the answer. 'A gift of God!' declared his father when several forty-gallon drums of South American rum washed up onto the strand, salvage from a ship sunk off the coast. The elder Doherty himself was first to sample them, scooping with his hands from a staved-in keg. 'It could bear salt water and still carry a sting,' he would fondly recall years after.

''Tis more the Devil's gift to you,' suggested the priest in departing their cottage one evening.

'The kingdom of God is but a vineyard!' roared his father in reply to the figure retreating down the lane. Yet it was not so much a matter of wine (or rum) but poteen for which the local curate refused absolution, sending you on to the Bishop instead. His father told Dermot once of a neighbour who unearthed a stoneware jar in the bog one evening while cutting turf alone. Five hours later the neighbour had need of more than the Bishop alone; indeed it would have taken St Patrick himself as the man screamed in terror at the snakes which writhed across the flagstones on his kitchen floor. After three sleepless nights his family sent him off to the mental where he did a fortnight's penance.

As he rinsed out his cup, Dermot noticed fresh signs of the mouse around the soap dish. Brushing them into the sink he debated buying a trap at the shop. Sure it was only eating the bar of green soap on the drainboard and had yet to get into any food. Maybe he should get a cat. Coming back to the table he saw the package once again. This time as he leaned over he wondered whether there was not a ticking sound within. With the fireplace poker in one hand, he gently pushed the package into the small shovel for ashes, scooping it up as delicately as if it were what an ill-mannered dog might deposit on your doorstep of a morning.

Once outside he placed it carefully on the backseat of his car.

The road into the village took Dermot past Paddy Cannon's cottage, the man's dog lying in front as Dermot drove by. Only a cur belonging to Cannon would choose the turned soil of an old potato patch to lie on, Dermot remarked to himself, instead of a grassy bank like any decent dog. The best that could be said about the poor animal's colouring were a few patches of off-white midst all the grey and black. Dermot could not recall in all of New York City a dog with a more scruffy demeanour, trailing great lengths of briar from its hindquarters as it skulked past you on the road. 'An animal reveals its master' suggests the old adage, and in the case of Cannon with his mug like a dog's breakfast, a saying had never rung so true.

'As stupid as the man is, he is not as stupid as he looks,' Dermot had told Andy in the toilet the night before. 'Christ, the face on him would crucify you, and him carrying on like that all night!'

'Did you see his nose?' Cannon was inquiring of McShane's niece helping her uncle out behind the bar.

'No, I don't believe I looked at it at all. I was looking all over the city, you know.'

That piqued him.

'Well, we're two different people then, you and I, because I climbed up there to look at his nose!'

And 'tis a pity you didn't stay up there thought Dermot to himself.

'What length was his nose would you think?' Cannon kept after the niece.

'I haven't a clue, really.'

'Well, you can guess, can't you?' hounded Cannon.

'Oh . . . four inches, then,' she said, wiping down the bar in front of him.

'Not at all, not at all!! Why your man over there has three inches himself!' Cannon exploded, gesturing toward Andy. 'Nelson would be no man at all with one that small!' Pausing, he drained his pint.

'For the love of God then, how long was his flaming nose?' burst out Dermot, drawn into the conversation despite himself.

'The nose on Nelson was nine inches long!' replied Paddy in triumph, setting down his glass.

'Not any longer it is!' said Dermot in a loud tone of satisfaction, as if the loss somehow diminished Cannon more than it did the Lord Admiral.

'Eejits!' shouted Paddy. 'Nothing but bloody eejits! The fools who blew him up were ignorant of the fact that Nelson was Irish! Irish he was, born in Dublin. A terrible thing, that. Why in years to come a statue like that would be worth the world!'

Ah, go home and give your dog a decent meal muttered Dermot into his pint. Turning away he glanced at the clock above the bar. Although the regulars scarcely noticed now, the clock brought yet an occasional comment from a stranger in the pub. From the five its thin second hand swept confidently to four-three-two where it slipped a fraction, struggled determinedly, then fell back to five where the ordeal began again. Yet it kept the hour well enough, and McShane saw little need of replacing it.

Booming from a table behind Dermot, Cannon's

voice floated across the pub to the bar, something about the river Liffey. As it was, Dermot cared little for Dublin, having been seduced by New York City before he ever saw her. At fourteen or so he and an older brother had come upon a deserted cottage on the mountain behind the glen. In its dark kitchen they found a wardrobe with its doors half hanging off. Inside were rows upon rows of neckties; all quite wide, some seemed to be of silk. There were stripes and diamonds and designs like lightening, and even a naked lady, but the strangest of all bore the image of another woman, this time fully clothed in a long robe, holding a torch high above her head. Behind her was the tallest building Dermot had ever seen; below were the letters NYC stitched in red thread. As his brother put the naked lady inside his shirt, Dermot knotted the New York tie around his neck and wore it down the mountain.

Parking the car outside McShane's, Dermot walked into the pub, feeling as he did his head suddenly begin to hammer like the heart of a criminal returning to the proverbial scene. Or in this case was it the victim? Shutting the door gently behind him, Dermot saw that McShane was alone in the place.

'How are you, Mot?' McShane inquired.

'If I shut my eyes they could bury me, Mickey.'

'It's not my whiskey that's done that to you,' McShane replied, pronouncing it 'fiskey' as they do in Donegal.

'Would you have any bread soda on sweet milk, Mickey? Something for the stomach?' When he mentioned the parcel the publican went out to the car for a look.

'You can't be too careful, Mot,' McShane exclaimed. 'We had a letter the other day from the wife's sister outside Belfast. There was a lad in the village there, a bit light you know, but harmless as a kitten. Retarded I guess you'd call it ... Always peeping out from behind bushes and that sort of carry-on. Everybody knew him of course—except the Brits who shot him dead one afternoon. Said he'd been acting "in a suspicious manner".'

ST CAMILLUS PATRON OF THE SICK AND DYING PRAY FOR US prompted the legend of a collection box on the bar in front of Dermot. As McShane continued Dermot thought how the voice could be his father's own, relating a similar story some fifty years before. Even when death had not involved the glory of the Republic, there had been a fascination with dying itself.

'You were often happy with the news of a wake,' remarked his father more than once, 'for it meant two square meals in those days, possibly more. And there would be a man at a table kept busy just cutting tobacco for the pipes.'

Indeed it was Camillus and not Patrick at all who deserved to be called Ireland's patron. Perhaps it was the years in America, or the loss of Maggie, but whatever the reason Dermot was sick of all the talk of dying, as if the confusion of death with nation and nation with death had somehow corrupted itself, like the plastic wreaths now laid on a grave where before there had been only whatever wild flowers might come up through the grass. He had never seen anything so hideous as those wreaths, all pinks and blues beneath a clear dome of plastic, like a frosted birthday cake in a bakery window. 'Sure and you will be pushing up daisies yourself once you are down long enough,' as his father often observed.

'You'd better take that package over to Willie Byrne at the Guards,' McShane suggested.

'I believe I'll take it to McGinley at the Post Office,' said Dermot as he finished his glass of milk. Willie's father and Dermot had been wee gassers together, always chumming around; summers they would climb the headland across the bay where after scrambling into the ruined tower the Byrne lad would trap the unfledged jackdaws. Whatever he caught he sold to a man from Belfast who split their tongues and taught them to talk like parrots. His son Willie, now one of two Gardai assigned to the village, made Dermot feel like a grandfather, much the same feeling as having a pint in the lounge beside the public bar at McShane's with its crowd of youngsters.

'Who in the world would want to blow you up, Mot?' asked John McGinley with a smile.

'I haven't a clue,' Dermot replied. He was beginning to feel a fool but still there was no explanation for the package.

'I'll have to ring the postmaster in Carrigaholt, as the parcel is registered,' McGinley explained.

'You're dead on,' said Dermot.

McGinley returned from the telephone. 'He doesn't remember your man Carr, but he still has the receipt. Anyhow, we've permission to open it. 'Tis a shame we haven't a bomb squad here,'

McGinley added with a laugh.

Dermot wished he would get on with it.

McGinley did, and before him on the counter lay Dermot's wristwatch, a gift from Maggie on his fiftieth birthday. He had given it a month ago to a friend in Letterkenny who knew another party whose pastime was watch-repair.

'God almighty!' said Dermot. 'I've no memory at all.'

'I may need to keep it for six months as evidence, Mot,' said McGinley with a louder laugh this time.

A few more stunts like this one and I'll be the village idiot thought Dermot driving home. He knew the codding he would take over the next few weeks but it did not really bother him. Except for whatever Paddy Cannon would think to say. Surely someone had split that tongue at the age of two and Cannon had not stopped talking since.

After supper he read for several hours. The summer wasn't so bad; what Dermot dreaded was the winter ahead with its endless nights. 'No point in going to bed when you can't sleep,' his father would say. 'No harder work than that can a man do.' Perhaps he would return to the States. He was luckier than Lear at least, as all of his daughters wanted him there.

Getting up from his chair he reached for the alarm clock above the hearth. He had seen signs of mackerel now for two days and there would be a filling tide early in the morning. 'Mackerel are the only fish in the sea to eat the human flesh of a drowned body,' his father had informed him once. With a mind like that, small wonder the man had drunk himself under.

Dermot set the alarm for a half hour before sunrise. Although he had bought the clock after the loss of Maggie who had always been first to rise, he seldom slept late now and he rarely used it. As he got into bed, his memory which could fail him over a month's time now took him back some thirty years; lying there he saw for a moment a summer's evening in the Bronx, an elevated train sweeping past, the fading sun as it fired the bricks along the tenement-lined street. Then the rustling of the mouse above the bedroom ceiling brought him back to Donegal. Through the open window he heard a corncrake, calling like some strange insect from the meadow below the lane. Two hours later he fell asleep.

One for Sorrow

'That's not a magpie, sure it's not,' startled by a burst of black and white feathers which flew across the road into an orchard of almond trees.

'A hoopoe,' Ailish said. 'They're African, with a red crest on their heads.' One of few island birds she knew, making her all the sadder that it heartened her little to share that knowledge with him. 'Two for joy,' she had tutored him only weeks before, spying from the upper level of their Dublin bus a pair of magpies in a garden off the Merrion Road near Sandymount. 'Three for marriage, four for a boy,' happy there were these things she could offer him.

It was early May, not yet high season in Majorca, and Ailish had managed to knock a thousand pesetas off the cost of a hired car. They could skimp later in the summer Owen said, though she would be working shortly, probably earning enough to keep them both. From Ireland it had seemed the perfect arrangement, she to work days with an Irish holiday outfit, Owen to write. The nights, they told each other, would take care of themselves.

'Would you think that flower was gorse?' he spoke again, pointing to the yellow shrub which seemed everywhere along the mountain road they hoped to follow as far as Deya. This time she hadn't the name and Owen grew quiet for a while. As if he'd caught himself using the Mediterranean to counter the strangeness between them, adapting island fauna and flora to point them back to Ireland.

When they stopped for a beer at a restaurant whose verandah overhung the sea, Owen walked over to take a closer look at the shrub. 'Yellow's the colour for getting things done quickly,' he had told her the week-end they met in Donegal, meaning her bright yellow vinyl boots which seemed cut from the same bolt as the yellow oilcloth on his kitchen table. The same yellow as the hired Fiat she now drove on these narrow, winding, Majorcan roads, wondering could she end it as quickly as they had begun.

They had met in Ireland that winter, the coldest the country had known in years. During her time with the Irish Tourist Board in New York, Ailish had worked with a large coloured poster of Glencullen above her desk. All mountains and sea, imagining always what it must be like. Born in Dublin, she had seen some of the west coast, though never as far north as Donegal. So this year when Mary had asked her to spend a week-end in that very village, she accepted gladly, thinking the cold would be no worse in a setting like that.

It was dark by the time they reached Glencullen. They had come the Sligo route, a brief stop at Drumcliff for Ailish to see the poet's grave, stopping again when the fanbelt gave out above Bundoran.

Asking their way near the village chapel, they heard a man with an American accent tell them he lived beside the cottage they sought. From the back seat Ailish could see little of the fellow who got in beside Mary, who talked surprisingly little for a Yank.

In Donegal long enough to have grown cautious as the locals, he said nothing about writing until a second cup of tea in the chalet belonging to Mary's uncle. Yes, he was of Irish extraction he answered Mary, but it was far back and he made little of it. He was thirty or so, a few years older than themselves. Thin, fair-haired, nearly a foot taller than Ailish's five foot two. Within twenty-four hours he told her that a marriage of five years had ended that autumn—as if knowing that within another twenty-four hours they would sleep together and he wanted her aware.

Yet all these numbers scarcely mattered, for her first sight of him seemed to remind her of only the happy times in her life, and she soon found it impossible to gauge just how long she had known him. Later that week in Eason's—to read in one of his stories what seemed shadows of their meeting—she would not know whether to laugh or cry. As if stories could be written both before and after the facts. Was it possible he had been there all along? Not alone the colour poster on Fifth Avenue that year in New York, but a sometimes fantasy that she would live someday with an artistic type, somewhere on the west coast of the island she had left for another south of Spain. She had never been able to see anything more than his hands, fingers thinner than her own. Reading an interview with painter or writer in the Sunday papers, she would try to picture herself with him.

Though his hands were fine enough, it would have wanted more than fantasy alone to lead to bed that week-end in Donegal. Saturday they walked the strand which ringed the village, climbed the mountain road to the tower set like a hat on Glen Head. Able to follow one another almost without words, they found themselves speaking in fragments much of the time, letting go the language when they sensed the other already knew or understood. 'Have you always been like that?' he asked her that Sunday night as they sat before the old range in the cottage he rented winters from an English painter, making pancakes bittersweet with orange rind in the batter.

'Always, but there's never been anyone to pick me up on it before.' She was relieved it was he who first spoke of being afraid, but told him she thought it would be all right.

'We'd be warmest in the loft,' he said, rummaging in the cupboard for a candle. They sat sharing a cigarette side by side, pillows propped against the wall. The post-coital scenario of countless films—only they had yet to touch. In the morning he told her of the sounds she had always made asleep, said that it had been like listening to the sea. Turning toward him she saw where traces of candle grease had spilled like semen onto the sheets.

'Psyche,' said Owen later as he made the bed. 'Wondering who her mystery lover was.' He was full of allusions like that. Not to impress she felt, but almost as a blind for them, saying that love in myth and legend always struck within five minutes—as if to excuse them both. It was a means of retreat she lacked, however; and she would leave for Dublin that afternoon with Mary in no way certain she was able for it all.

It was a fortnight before they saw each other again. This time Ailish took the Express bus from Dublin to Donegal Town. She spent the night in a hotel on the Diamond, next morning rode the provincial bus to the fishing port where she changed to another that ended its run at Glencullen. At a pub in the village she had a glass of Harp, wondering should she turn back. When Owen thanked her for coming clear across Ireland, she told him it would have been no harder, no easier, to journey across the street. That night it froze so hard that ice coated the scullery window both inside and out, a lace curtain drawn against the sea below the road. At breakfast they talked for the first time of his joining her in Spain.

Shortly after, Owen came to Dublin, intending to stop for a few days with musician friends in Sandycove before he flew to America for a month. Had either of them suspected the magic to have been Donegal alone, Dublin soon set them straight, the few days lengthening into most of March. Later it would seem impossible to Ailish that she had worked those weeks, her job a temporary appointment with the *Bórd* secured through a friend from her New York days. Still she managed to make the office most mornings, almost grateful now for the tedium of the guidebooks she was asked to update. Targeted especially, as they said in the trade, at the North American market. 'Have you any idea on the number of American bed-nights?' Mary asked for badness at tea-break, pleased as most of us are with a role in another's romance.

'Not a clue,' laughed Ailish, caring little what the other girls made of it all.

Somehow she managed at home also, these three months in Ireland what she gave her parents each year, returning from Majorca to the small terraced house in Rathmines, an abode she could not abide for more than a week. Her mother ventured out less each year, her father quieter each visit, threatening to vanish entirely into the murmur of radio and telly which played from morning to night. There was no need to come home, her married sisters who all lived in Dublin told her. But then this year there seemed to have been reason enough.

There in Dublin the tapestry of her past first glimpsed in Donegal now trailed into the everyday. With Owen in a pub one evening on Eden Quay, she heard a song play that years before in Spain had brought her to tears for no reason. It had played in her head alone that first time, suggesting there was someone who truly loved her, only somehow she had missed him. 'Alguien me ama, Paco,' she wept to her Majorcan fellow of that season, seated entirely clothed on the edge of the bath where he had found her with her head in her hands.

That even then it had been Owen she could accept—if only because she felt no need to insist upon the conjunction, as if proof itself were sometimes of little account in trials of the heart. In fact there was proof of more than she cared to confront: things coinciding past coincidence to reveal, if not a larger loom at work, surely a higher incidence of the bizarre which now elbowed its way into her day and night.

Given a horse in the Gold Cup by Owen in a dream, she shunned a bookie out of vague scruple, betting against her father to make a pound seventy on a ten pence piece. At Mary's flat where they stole the odd afternoon, a window blind flew up with a sound like gunfire, a framed print falling simultaneously two rooms away. 'The wind,' Owen offered, and perhaps it was.

The near banality of such circumstance served only to make it all that more credible, as if the commonplace and incidental can at times persuade more readily than the fantastic. Nor is it always easy, as Ailish discovered, to know which you might prefer. Feeling one afternoon as if glass might shatter, they walked down to the water in Dun Laoghaire. There at the end of a small concrete pier in the March wind they went astray. There seemed to be no way out, trapped between train tracks and the sea, the numbered lanes on the car park no help at all. 'Seachráin,' she heard Owen say as she cried quietly into his coat, giving it the Irish he had heard in Donegal.

'Had we a hat to turn on our heads,' he said later, 'we'd have been out of it sooner.' Or so they held in Connemara, he explained. More ways than string alone to beat the Minotaur.

'It was the cold, Owen,' she told him, and they let it lie at that. Neither one especially eager to be again so mesmerized, if only in memory.

'An arm and a leg,' he said later that evening when she asked what they had wanted for the room. Unable to find a phone kiosk south of the Canal in working order, they had given up on a guest house, ending up in a hotel on Pembroke Road instead.

'A good job they didn't know we'd give more limbs than that,' she replied, drawing a smile from him as she drew the heavy curtains. 'Will you come in?' she asked from the bed as Owen struggled with a coat hanger, thinking how often it was his own talk that seemed all that mattered. The hair below her belly soft as feathers, herself both swan and Spartan girl. It was not so much a hat they wanted, she could consider at moments like these. More a string of coloured floats, like those at a lake-side, something guaranteed to keep them at their proper depth.

'Is there any sexual fantasy I should know about?' Owen joked the next morning, the bedclothes over them from a mutual shyness which, because shared, seemed to Ailish no less intimate than their lovemaking.

'Perhaps, but it's not for publication,' she laughed, telling him of a dream in which she sat in the back seat of a taxi somewhere in New York City. The driver, a man in his fifties, finds without turning his head the hem of her ankle-length skirt.

'Ligottage,' Owen told her in turn as she rang her mother to say she had spent the night at Mary's. Later to write him in America that the house in Rathmines had her fit to be tied, she would laugh and underline the words.

Saint Patrick's Day fell Saturday the week-end before Owen departed Dublin. Heavy snow fell also, burying much of the country from the Curragh west. The Sandycove folk had gone to Cork, leaving them the house. It snowed off and on in Dublin, the slush on the pavement a grey echo of the sky. There were no birds visible from the Number 14 bus to Phoenix Park, the bare trees black above the bandstand which seemed about to slide down its knoll. In the aviary at the Zoological Gardens too many birds, the air close with their clamour and confinement.

While they ate lunch the snow began to blow again, driving a peacock and peahen who had the freedom of the grounds to shelter in the covered porch near their table. As they watched to see if the cock might spread his tail, two children dashed up the steps, shouting from the storm. Trapped by the commotion the birds flew in panic at the door, suspended for a moment like brightly coloured fish against an aquarium glass. Leaving the restaurant they saw a handful of people as excited as the children, pointing across the pond which lay below the slope of the path.

Ailish saw it first, an outsized simian form moving down the small park below the ape-house. She wanted to run but Owen took her elbow, pointing out the water that lay between. There was not a person on foot in sight, no one but the ape and a blue van which drove slowly back and forth on the road below the animal: two primates at a game of cat and mouse.

The ape seemed almost to ape itself. In name and nature as the saying has it, arms swinging in wild exaggeration, shoulders slung so low that its hands brushed the snow as it walked. The van meantime never varied, its movement in response to the creature's vector as impersonal as the white line on a carriageway.

The tableau lasted what seemed an eternity, the giant figure dark against the snow, the grey waters below flecked with flamingoes on the nearer shore. Then, turning suddenly, the ape retreated up the hill, climbing the iron paling of the fence as easily as its keepers might step off a kerb. Without a backward glance it pushed open the swinging doors of its house, appeared briefly in the large glass, then dropped from view.

The small group on the hill opposite were slow to scatter. Like theatregoers who hold their seats at the final curtain, reluctant to let illusion loose. Most of them headed for the ape-house, Owen and Ailish also, laughing at the zoo personnel who now appeared on the run with a net and poles, sceneshifters rushing up with forgotten props.

Once there they began to disassemble the set instead, sweeping up soil from an overturned large potted palm. The orang-utan sat watching all the activity, tapping a thin bamboo rod on the concrete floor as an attendant removed the broken section of copper pipe on which it had swung across the deep pit that served as the sole barrier between its space and the viewing corridor with its swinging doors. Up close the ape did not look half as big, though still a fair size. Its long arms out of all proportion to its body, orange hair and bald belly.

'He didn't mean any harm, did he?' Owen said as they stood arm in arm.

'No more than any of us,' Ailish answered, feeling again as if a pageant had ended: that they were being handed back a familiar world in black and white.

By evening however, any melancholy had vanished, memory having chosen the peacock's plumage over its panic, emotion as often rearranged as recollected in tranquillity. They laid a fire in the Sandycove sitting room, had tea and sandwiches before the TV news which kept the secret of Phoenix Park, featuring footage of the St. Patrick's Day parade led that morning by the mayor of Dublin, Ohio. As it happened, the escaped ape never made the headlines. Monday was a Bank Holiday without papers. Tuesday's were full of coverage of the thousands expected to march that day through Dublin in a demonstration against taxes. The protest was larger than anticipated, shutting down the city centre and delaying Owen's plane to America by several hours.

'You seem blue,' he ventured that afternoon when they at last reached Deya, a massive cliff-face rising this time above the terrace of their café.

'It's a bit confusing, coming back here, then having you arrive.'

'Give it time.'

'It was only three weeks or so, us in Ireland,' Ailish ventured herself.

'Six weeks,' he corrected her. 'If you believe in calendars.'

'Maybe you have to, after all,' thinking how he had dropped that morning the outsized alarm clock she had packed in Dublin, an old-fashioned model with two bells and a clapper on top. 'It still works,' he had apologised for his clumsiness, the glass cracked but not shattered. 'Would you wind it, pet?' she asked from the bathroom of the efficiency flat. The house she had hoped for in a nearby village was already let. The apartment belonging to her holiday company would be vacant for a few weeks yet.

They sat that afternoon for an hour in the sun at Deya, drinking Cerveza San Miguel which Owen said tasted like Mexican beer. Saying in other words that there were other places, should Majorca not work out. The tables were about half full, the talk a mixture of French, English, and Mallorquin, small children chasing a smaller dog and black cat across the flagstones. Deya now boasting at least one popular rock band as well as its aging English poet in residence—whose collection of Greek myth Owen had given Ailish the evening he arrived.

She had gifts for him in turn that night, his Irish pipe tobacco with its scent like soap, a T-shirt from the *Bórd* emblazoned with the adaptation of a slogan she had first seen in New York selling Jewish bread. 'You Don't Have to be Irish to Love Ireland,' he read backwards, holding the shirt up to the mirror. 'You don't have to be that to love Irish either,' he offered, only Ailish had left the bedroom to make them tea.

She had been almost an hour late in meeting his flight earlier that evening. Twice missing the airport road from the carriageway so that she had to double back into Palma, unable to untrack herself. Looking for a clock in the airport terminal she saw Owen leaning against a wall.

'Taxi?' she asked him before he saw her there, surprised to find him exactly as she remembered, perhaps somewhat paler. 'You're white yourself,'

Owen told her in the car, as though she had spoken her thought aloud.

That had not changed. Nor was it a question of Mexico over Majorca she knew, any more than Dublin had differed from Donegal. 'We'd better go if we're to have the car back on time,' she said, shivering a little now that the sun had left the terrace. They pooled pesetas for a tip, took the inland route from Deya back to Palma which cut the time in half.

She left Owen at the flat, telling him that she needed to stop by her holiday agency on the way to the airport to drop off the hired car. This time she had no problem finding the airport road, pulling into the carpark just as the rental man was locking up his tiny shed. At the Departures Terminal she hailed a taxi for the trip back into the city, staring out the window at the irrigation windmills on the flats along the road.

'Are you on holiday?' the taxista asked as they turned onto the avenue along the sea, the old cathedral on their left.

'No, I'm working,' she told him.

'Como una guia?'

'Yes, as a guide, more or less.'

Speaking more rapidly, he began to tell Ailish of a guide who was his fare the year before. She had the most beautiful legs; her legs were still a vision in his mind. 'Everybody has something beautiful about them,' he added. 'With you it's your eyes. Such lovely eyes.'

'Well,' she laughed, able to see the block of flats in the distance.

Would she have a coffee with him? Everyone with some beauty: 'A mouth, a nose, the hands,' he catalogued. Had she a boy-friend?

'You don't have to pay,' he said when they reached the building.

'How much is it?' Ailish asked, annoyed more by the innuendo than his persistence.

'Often if someone cannot pay, I let it go.'

'What do I owe?' she asked again, by now outside the taxi.

Three hundred pesetas he told her.

'A coffee, nothing more. Only twenty minutes.'

'I can't; I've someone waiting.'

'A kiss, then. Your eyes,' he repeated.

Laughing, she leaned down and kissed him through the window. At that he pulled up the handbrake and jumped out of the cab. 'Just a coffee, only twenty minutes,' he pleaded, a few grey hairs visible at the collar of his shirt.

More than startled, Ailish told him no. She turned up the steps without looking back and he did not follow. Shaken, she decided on a coffee after all, though she made certain the taxi had left before she went down the steps to a sandwich shop across the street. Seated at the counter however, she began to laugh. There had been no real danger she knew. The incident, such as it was, having played itself out—if not in downtown Manhattan, only yards from her building, the area lit by both lamps and the last of the sun. 'He hadn't meant any harm,' she told herself, evoking as she did an outsized figure on a snow-covered hill.

Suddenly it seemed to make perfect sense that she was leaving Owen, as if she recognised in these

103

recent days something of the colours from that afternoon in Phoenix Park. Only now she felt that those watching had shared beyond an interlude alone, all of them hoping that the ape might manage what they would not. Uncaged, to continue into whatever else lies beyond. If not for those watching a question of iron bars or wire mesh, then a string of coloured floats, the luminescent circle of a clock, the lines on a calendar. Whatever one uses to stay at a familiar depth.

She thought of Owen, Glencullen, Phoenix Park, her taximan, setting them down like coins on the counter. A lump sum that suggested fantasy and dream sometimes ask not only that you believe, but that you choose as well. If so, perhaps some day she would consider herself at least lucky in the knowledge that dreams do come true. No matter that they bring their own reality with them, sometimes not unlike a cold wind or wet snow underfoot. But for now it was enough to see clearly her next move.

Opening her bag to pay for the coffee, she saw the paperback Owen had given her. He would do all right, she knew. That for him it was a string of brightly coloured words and the names of things, allusion when illusion failed. He would do fine she told herself again as she waited for the lift with a German couple and child, all with ice cream. She smiled back at them, remembering now that she had seen them earlier on the pavement not far from her taxi. The daughter being photographed holding a lion cub—one of several sorry animals whose owners worked the waterfront.

'Mimosa,' Owen told her when she came in. As if

to prove her right, having already discovered the name of the yellow bush. 'Seven for tales that will never be told' he would write of them in a year's time, though now he sat head in hands on the edge of the bed, listening to her say that she could not get it going, that she had never meant him any harm.

Vanishing Boundaries

Covering the fireplace with a sheet of newspaper, Harris heard the fire catch with a faint murmur, then grow with a tiny roar like a sheet of rain approaching at a distance. Although he was two weeks in the cottage, he still needed half an hour before the turf took and held the flame from twisted newsprint and dried fuchsia. The fire shared the cottage with him, its presence like that of a cat always in the same corner. Sometimes as he sat reading at night the wind would drop, and Harris would lift his head, suddenly aware of the muted muttering from the fire as if it had just then spoken to him.

He fashioned each day around the fire, spending afternoons along the strand searching for kindling. Some days he brought back a fence post, or an odd beam that the sea had spit up the night before, and borrowing a saw from Kilpatrick he warmed himself cutting logs for the fire that evening. He sensed nothing primal in his hunt along the strand, nothing sacred or ceremonial as he knelt before the hearth. If anything, there was a science involved, and Harris set about to master it, regulating the flue in the fireplace fender as if it were the boiler of some steamship. Even that would have been a fanciful comparison for Harris, were it not for the volume of Conrad on the shelf above the hearth. Meantime the fire soon claimed the tiny hairs along his knuckles.

Despite the simplicity of his daily routine, Harris focused on the tasks as if they held a hidden fascination, as if the fellow who washed his breakfast dishes or his shirt were in some sense a stranger. His life back home involved a routine also, only there the repetition served as framework for the people who filled his day: the hours he kept at the office or hospital marshalled his incoming patients much as the squares in the appointment book which held their names. Now he passed the hours alone, exchanging an idle word along with some coins for milk and groceries in the small village nearby, the only one for miles along the road which followed the Irish coast.

For the first week it seemed he had never known anything so beneficial as his isolation. It was the first real vacation he had taken since entering medical school ten years ago, and the feeling of solitude after the years filled with people was as a balm or lotion applied to his very skin. He went down one evening to the pub beside the post office, but understood nothing of the man next to him at the bar who exhaled with a continual mutter indistinguishable from his speech. Withdrawing to a table, Harris gave in gradually to the hypnotic glow of bottles behind the bar, drifting along on the cross-currents of conversation which floated over to his corner.

He called one afternoon on Kilpatrick, who had

rented him the cottage for three weeks in November without passing any comment on his choice of season. Harris had gone to borrow a saw but accepted an invitation to tea from the old man's wife. He found it hard to gauge Kilpatrick's exact age: what looked like years might well be the work of wind, weather, or illness. Harris guessed that the farmer had probably suffered a stroke, reading the slurred speech and facial muscles much as Kilpatrick would the sea and sky. As the old man talked one hand moved without ceasing over the fabric of his armchair as if touch might recall something that memory alone could not.

The farmer asked him to compare Boston to Donegal, and Harris said that there were a lot of Irish in both. There are more in Boston, Kilpatrick replied. His wife telling Harris that all the children were either in England or America. Somewhat later the farmer began to talk about rabbits. They had overrun the glen five years before, eating grain, gardens, everything. Kilpatrick often had rabbit for dinner then. Skinned and gutted, he would tie them up with an onion inside overnight, bake them the next day. The onion took off all taste of grass. Then someone brought in myxamatosis and wiped them out.

'It was June and you would see the rabbits dead on the ditches, crawling along the road, their heads the size of a small cabbage,' Kilpatrick formed one with his hands. 'If there was a puddle on the road, they'd have their heads in it, for that was what it was—a burning and swelling in the brain.'

'The wonders of science,' said Harris without wanting to. He disliked the facile irony—if there were no more rabbits, there was no tuberculosis left either—but he had suddenly imagined the lane strewn with rabbits, all with large leafy heads.

'It was cruel,' Kilpatrick said, 'but they were cruel to the farmer as well.'

There had been improvements, of course. As Kilpatrick took him slowly down to the byre to see the two cows, he talked about the warble fly that laid its eggs beneath the hide, leaving a hole to bedevil the tanner. But now a man came once a year with a solution to be poured along the animal's backbone.

To Harris the glen seemed another world. The play of colour on the sea and hills shifted within minutes, turning the mountain across the bay from red to green to grey. Rainbows were commonplace; to his amazement they often appeared in pairs, like brushstrokes along the mountain opposite. Staring at a sky where the heavy overcast had broken to reveal orange patterns as flat as paint upon a wall, he teased from memory an explanation read years before about the properties of colour and light . . . 'when complementary colours of equal value and little intensity are placed side by side, their boundaries vanish.' He wondered if it were only inevitable that after ten years of medicine he should ascribe theories of cause and effect even unto sunsets. He spent hours walking the highlands above the cottage, where he encountered no one but black-faced sheep who seemed to have some innate sense of the dramatic, appearing suddenly silhouetted along a ridge as empty as the others moments before. Once he came upon three ewes lying within a small hollow, arranged with all the unreality of a fifteenth century Flemish scene. As if in agreement, the sheep disdained to scatter at his approach.

The land thereby proved as elusive as the sea and sky. Lured by the strange loveliness of the brown and barren hills, he would be driven home by a gale whose savageness belied that gentle seduction of only an hour before. Each afternoon on the strand he found new contours and line along the sand he had crossed the day before, shaped afresh by wind and tide. Along the hightide mark lay scattered clusters of flotsam, each one a collage of twigs, seaweed, dried foam, and shells. Dissatisfied as any artist with its creation, the tide rearranged the tangled piles twice daily, though Harris could read nothing but randomness midst all the patterns. After a week he recognised old friends which, having washed up beyond the reach of succeeding tides, lay unredeemed by the sea: a woman's boot of orange and black stripes, a broken tub of purple plastic, a rotten turnip. One afternoon he found a fence post lying among patches of brown foam like suds of stout. It was a solid piece for burning, marred only by a thin layer of sand and a few barnacles, with none of the spongy feel of waterlogged wood.

As the saw dropped the first section, however, Harris smelled the seaworms—even before he saw their bore holes through the centre. He knocked the log on a rock and a worm oozed out at the cut end, a transparent envelope of jelly with its viscera visible within. The smell was strong, of dead fish and something else.

His feeling of surprise lasted into the evening. Its persistence reminded Harris of a similar uneasiness upon once discovering someone asleep on a cot amid all the rubble of the basement in the apartment where he had lived as a medical student. In those days medicine had seemed to him primarily a science of symptoms: once properly divined, one need seldom be surprised by what lay beneath the surface. It was this certainty in medicine that most attracted him, and he had shown little interest in its more nebulous branches, such as psychiatry. Concepts of body and mind were easy to handle, when he bothered to, as solid as blocks of turf. Unlike many of his classmates he refused to experiment with drugs—to his mind the idea of taking a pill *to produce* symptoms was entirely backwards, if not absurd.

After a year in a public health programme in Central America, Harris returned to Boston, a specialist in internal medicine. Over the next three years he shared an office practice with an older doctor, working afternoons at the out-patient clinic of a city hospital. It was only in this period that the certainties of medical school began to fade somewhat. In the tropics you found parasites at the source of most disorders—or gross deficiencies in diet. But now Harris seldom uncovered such clear-cut causes. His private patients described their symptoms—lethargy, nerves, loss of appetite—as if they were the affliction itself. At the clinic he ran the same series of barium X-rays on his poorer patients, but often wondered if he could not read more in complaints of overwork and similar laments. One patient had difficulty distinguishing his ulcer from a son who moved home each time he lost his job. Even the heavy drinking that brought on certain stomach disorders seemed more another symptom than any initial cause, some strange blossom on a plant whose roots remained hidden from view. At times Harris wondered if he should not have chosen surgery, where at least you ended up with something you could hold in your hand. He remembered with envy the nights on duty as an intern in an emergency room where the broken bones and lacerations arrived already certified, as it were, in the data of the accompanying police report with its specifics of an automobile accident or knifing.

That night he did not burn the worm-riddled wood. Instead, he laid on the turf another find from the strand. The piece had been heavy, over four feet long, and curved at either end like a rib. Cut, its cross-section revealed a bone-dry grain as dark as any wood that Harris had seen. When he showed Kilpatrick the timber, the old man asked where on the beach it had lain.

'On the far end.'

'It's from a ship that washed up there,' Kilpatrick told him. 'Over a hundred years ago.'

'Is there more beneath the sand?'

'Aye. The wind uncovers a piece now and then, like what you have there. The wood is black oak.'

The farmer's story of a shipwreck put Harris in mind of his man Conrad. He wondered what kind of ship had broken up off the southwest coast of Donegal. Was there possibly a thread that led to the author himself, one of its crew who might have shipped out on another vessel that earlier or later carried the writer who had himself gone to sea? With an amused chuckle Harris cut himself off in mid-flight. Unaccustomed as he was to such fancy, Ireland in November seemed scarcely suited for making a romantic of him. If that morning's storm which caught him on the mountain possessed a fury worthy of Conrad's world, it had also soaked Harris to the bone, driving him cold and miserable back to the cottage.

The black oak burned for hours: a strange blue flame that stuttered inside a border of orange. 'When complementary colours of equal value and high intensity are placed side by side, their boundary vibrates.' The colours themselves, he decided, were simply a matter of sodium chloride and whatever else had soaked up from the sea. He went to bed without banking the embers, so that as the wind blew up in gusts around the cottage, the fire responded: shadows of flame dancing through the door onto his bedroom wall. His last thought before sleep was that the murmur of the sea beyond mimicked the sound of a shell held to an ear.

The following morning as he stood shaving Harris saw the rash, running from his bicep down to his forearm, a string of red patches like an archipelago along his skin. Putting his razor down, he examined the arm with a professional disinterest. Unable to recall its Latin name, he saw quite clearly the page of a text which described its symptoms. He had nothing more than a case of ringworm, though that was badly named, for it was not the work of worms but fungi. Kilpatrick had a more colourful name when Harris showed him the arm that afternoon.

'Cattle scab. Curran can cure you of that.'

'Is Curran the vet?'

Indeed not. Rather the seventh son of a seventh

son who lived on a town-land several miles outside the village. Kilpatrick departed shortly, as if embarrassed at having told the visitor such a thing.

Harris remained in the lane, trying to remember a nursery rhyme about a man with seven wives. Why not call on Curran, he mused—as memory moved from a child's book of verse to a room-mate in medical school who once tried to explain why he took a pill that made concrete bubble before his eyes like oatmeal on a stove. No one in Ireland knew that he was a doctor. Nor was there any question of ethics involved: physician heal thyself belonged to Shakespeare, not Hippocrates. Besides, he thought with a laugh, he'd have one hell of a time trying to locate the proper salve in Donegal.

If he were a rationalist, he wasn't a bigot about it, unlike his uncle who walked out whenever his aunt mentioned the tennis court. Startled by what she described as an unearthly scream, her doubles partner had dropped her racket in the middle of her service. His aunt had heard nothing at all. That evening the woman received a cable from Ireland that her mother had died, the hour of death that afternoon in Dublin tallying with the hour for which they'd reserved the tennis court that morning in Massachusetts. Psychology had its domain, as Harris had come to appreciate since medical school, but the explanation offered of a hallucination occasioned by anxiety over a mother's illness did not of itself detract from what Harris considered a fine story. As to the timing involved, well, the world was large enough that no such coincidence would prove even more astounding. Hysteria! had been his uncle's only comment.

Harris easily found the farm, set back from the road by a lane with shelter belts of pine along either side, found Curran behind a small byre turning the soil with a broken spade. He leaned against a wall as the American talked of nothing, of the weather, his holidays. As Harris talked, he stared at the other man's hands. Out of all proportion to the rest of his body: large, brown, gnarled, they resembled the roots of a tree that, pushing through the soil, weather to look like branches themselves.

Finally mentioning Kilpatrick, Harris showed Curran his arm. When the farmer said nothing, it made Harris feel suddenly naked—as if he had exposed far more than his arm alone. He was a fool to have come.

At last Curran pointed down to the ground where Harris saw an earthworm disappearing beneath a sod.

'Pick it up and leave it in your hand.'

Together they watched it wriggle around his palm.

'Now place it in mine,' Curran directed.

The worm writhed once, then ceased moving. Lay motionless, limp, dead. As Curran moved to place his hand over the patchwork along his arm, Harris never even thought to warn him that the fungi were contagious. He felt the heat in the other man's touch.

On the road back to the village he saw something that looked like a rabbit bound behind a wall. Probably a cat he decided. Stopping at the shop he bought an antibiotic ointment, for simple bacterial infections, useless against fungi.

Two days later the arm was clear, as though its archipelago had sunk back into the sea overnight.

At breakfast the milk turned his tea the colour of rain. As he threw the leaves over the fuchsia hedge beyond the kitchen door, Harris saw that the wind had shifted, the clouds now rolling out to sea like a film running in reverse. The bay a single heavy green swell, hung-over from a storm far out to sea the night before. When he stepped inside, he found that the newspaper taped across the fireplace to create a draught had ignited, leaving a window of smouldering edges which framed the hearth. A piece of ash floated across the kitchen on broken wings, slowly dissolving into tiny points of fire like the markings of an exotic butterfly.

He went late that afternoon to the strand. The wind had shifted to the west again, and the sea was up; more angry now than sluggish, with waves the colour of cabbage in boiling milk. A flock of blackbirds whirled over the water, then swooped inland —dropping below the skyline they blended into the mountain and gathering dark so as to disappear, then shot up again like a shovelful of wood chips flung into the sky. The clouds out to sea trailed dirty streaks of rain which fell toward the horizon like giant kite tails, the sands empty apart from two barrel staves painted red.

Harris had almost reached the path back up to the road when he saw the sea bird over the water. It flew with its long black neck stretched level before it, reminding him of a loon he'd seen once off the coast of Maine. Or heard rather—that remarkable laughter that seemed to play tag with the late afternoon sun on the waves. He heard nothing now but the roar of the surf, the bird turning great circles above the sea. Until diving low, it tucked in its wings and settled between two crests, to remain there rising and falling on the swell. Then, though nothing changed, for a moment the scene seemed to shift—as if the bird had somehow gentled the ocean itself. Startled, Harris stared across the strand where the once raging waves now carried the cormorant like a cradle.

Turning quickly, Harris hurried up the path. If anything, the wind against his back had risen. By the time he reached the road night had fallen, the stream that he passed each day into the village sounding much louder in the dark. Or was it much darker in the loud? Why not synaesthesia as well he thought; rhyming nicely with anaesthesia, perhaps he would take up acupuncture along with faith-healing upon his return? And vacation next year in China where at least there would be far more people about. The solitude which he had welcomed so at first had obviously begun to chafe. After supper he fell asleep in front of the hearth. When the wind awoke him in the early morning, he saw the fire down to a level bed of embers that winked back at him in the dark.

The Answer Man

The milking done, Andy McShane paused by the door to the byre, looking down to the sea two hundred yards below the cottage. The sun upon the water seemed to have turned the sea to stone, the entire bay a slab of grey slate unbroken by any movement. On the far side a few flecks of white marked the gulls resting there on the rocks. Turning away Andy entered the cottage where his morning cup of tea awaited him. Inside the kitchen Mary took the pail from him, remarking on how little the cow gave now that she was within weeks of calving.

Her comment recalled for Andy the man from the Ministry of Agriculture who had visited some eight months before, accompanied by £15,000 worth of cattle, all keeping nicely in a vat of liquid nitrogen in the front seat of his car.

'Is she in there?' he'd asked Andy, pointing toward the byre.

'She is,' replied Andy before entering the kitchen to tell Mary to put on the kettle for the thermos jug in which the pipette of frozen semen would be warmed for fifteen seconds. Though denounced at first by the village priest, artificial insemination seemed a marvel of science to Andy, offering the offspring of fine and famous bulls, some of whom were fifteen years dead. He recited to himself the various breeds available, Aberdeen, Angus, Charolais, Hereford, Friesian, feeling a sense of pleasure in his knowledge as if in possessing their names he somehow possessed them all, though he had chosen only a Dairy Short Horn as the future calf.

Since Mary was at the sink in the entryway, Andy rose from the table to fill his cup. 'More tea or I'll appear!' his father had often advised his mother half in jest, but if there were seldom anger in the McShane kitchen now, there was little enough banter either. The liveliness of their courtship had not survived past the first childless years of their marriage, and now in their middle fifties, he and Mary had seen that marriage reduce itself to a series of responses nearly as regular as the seasons which ruled their small farm on the coast of Donegal.

Indeed certain memories seemed more the fragments of another life to Andy, the lad who wrote their names in giant letters along the strand was surely someone with more daring than he, no matter that the filling tide had within minutes swept their secret from the sands. Yet it would take more than the seas alone to keep a courtship from a village the size of Glenmalin, and when the summer months brought the traditional outings to Rathlin O'Birne, it was by then common knowledge that he and Mary comprised a couple among the young people who took an accordion and supper to the island where they danced long into the summer evening.

The cat against his leg begging for her breakfast brought Andy back to his own. He and Mary shared no outings now: the wife spent a night at Bingo in the Church Hall, he an occasional night at the pub, the both of them to Mass on Sunday of course, only Andy walked down early while Mary was lifted by a neighbour.

Perhaps it was not hunger but affection with the cat this morning thought Andy, wondering if she were in heat again. She never missed, nor did the male cats of the townland fail to appear, yet in seven years she had mothered nothing. He remembered reading recently that given a chance, the male cat would kill the kittens, for as long as the mother nursed she would not come into heat. McShane read more than most in the village: newspapers, old magazines, sometimes staying up into the wee hours of the morning with the photo supplements to the Sunday papers or an odd book. If not a critical reader he was not entirely without scepticism either, and this morning he wondered to himself whether it was true about the cats. Perhaps the Yank next door would know? There had been no signs of life in their cottage yet that morning as he had gone about the milking.

Their new neighbours were an American couple, renting from a shopkeeper in the village the old cottage which shared the hillside with McShane's. 'You wouldn't find their kind during the bleeding period here,' observed Andy in the pub as he often did of visitors who came on holiday to the Glen for the summer months. 'They wouldn't stick it in January, no way.'

When he learned the man was a writer, McShane

grew even more determined to keep his distance. 'I won't be talking to that party for fear he'd put something I said into a book,' he allowed to Mary one evening. Then hearing it was not stories but history the man wrote, Andy relaxed somewhat. After proving themselves decent enough neighbours over several weeks, the man stopped McShane one morning to inquire of the difference between the two Dublin papers sold in the village.

'A varying interpretation of the same lies,' was Andy's response to which the Yank had laughed at length. Shortly thereafter he and Taylor moved beyond exchanged greetings to extended conversation, sometimes talking for an hour at a time, Andy leaning on his haying rake in the meadow above the sea where the Yank was headed with an expensive fishing rod and the wrong gear for either pollock or mackerel.

Taylor was from Boston where riots over black children attending school in Irish-American neighbourhoods had recently made the Dublin papers. McShane himself had no experience with people of colour, the only black faces in Glenmalin those on the collection box for the African Missions in the pub, emblazoned with an appeal to *Put Something in for the Black Babies*. The black babies stared out of a photograph, their eyes oversized in faces shrunken by famine, itself no stranger to Glenmalin. When Taylor suggested the problem in Boston was not only a conflict of race but one of class also, it prompted McShane to turn the conversation to poetry.

'Did you know Bobbie Burns is held by some to be the first Socialist?'

'Really?' Taylor replied.

'Aye. They reckon the lines about "the best laid plans" are indications of Socialist thought. Marx, I believe, mentions Burns in his writings,' Andy added, encouraged by his listener's apparent interest. He wondered if the American ever wrote poetry himself but held back from asking such a personal question.

Indeed the news that the visitor was a writer had attracted McShane as much as it had given him pause. If one usually learned something from a foreign visitor, if only a queer way they had (he'd once met a Swiss who made sandwiches of bananas), the prospect of a learned neighbour offered even more. For McShane was a man who hungered after knowledge, taking a pleasure in facts and statistics such as others might from a fine meal. Twisting up newsprint to lay beneath the turf, McShane would marvel that flame could reduce in moments the details of famine, wars and nations to ashes on the grate.

Like many in Glenmalin Andy left at an early age the village school where one learned little from the master except to hate him more each year. 'You wouldn't abuse a brute animal how he'd abuse you,' McShane confided to Taylor one afternoon. 'Had you relations for years back with an impediment in their speech or a limp in their walk, he'd toss it up to you. If your uncle stuttered he'd imitate it for the class. Let him be lame and he would show you how he walked!'

Aroused by a subject McShane had a way of emphasizing each word he uttered like beating on a drum. For Taylor the weeks in Donegal were developing something of an eye for fine detail in a man long accustomed to dealing almost entirely in historical abstractions. At that moment noting how the white stubble along the weathered cheeks of his neighbour formed a pattern startlingly similar to that of the tan herringbone jacket Andy had on, as if the sun had thrown its weave upon the farmer's face as it will clouds upon the water.

That same afternoon Taylor invited McShane in for a cup of tea: Andy accepting, surprising both Taylor and himself. 'Good, that!' commented the farmer on a piece of sweetbread which Taylor's wife served him, leaving it nearly untasted upon his plate. Although he heaped sugar into his tea, he distrusted its presence in baking of any kind. Taylor's wife soon disappeared into a bedroom, leaving her husband and McShane to discuss the South American soccer team trapped in the Andes, the account of whose survival through cannibalism was currently being carried in serial form in a Sunday paper.

'Any conversation I attempt with him is stillborn at the start,' she complained after McShane departed, still unsettled by the farmer's obvious discomfort in her presence.

'He's a shy man,' replied Taylor, helping himself to the cake Andy had left. Indeed cautious was the village's own word for McShane who despite the solitude within his marriage had few close companions throughout Glenmalin. Still there existed in the community a kind of respect for the bits and bobs of information which filled his talk, for Andy's nature was not that of a braggart or blowhard. Yet if he were cautious with his own, small wonder that he managed not at all with the young American woman presently his neighbour.

Having thrown the cat out of the cottage, McShane started down the lane, noting the smoke now coming from the American's cottage. Opening the gate fashioned from an old bed-spring, he headed for the lower end of the meadow where the few strands of barbed wire to keep the cow from the sea were in sorry need of repair. Heavy with calf, it would hardly do to have her slip through them in search of greener pasture, and risk losing her on the rocks which tumbled down to the water. As he passed the tramcocks that would feed her and her calf through the winter, McShane reflected that the same wondrous science to double his herd was, in fact, a two-edged sword, for the American and his wife in their early thirties were a couple as childless as Mary and he after thirty years of marriage, though for themselves it had been a matter of God's will alone. In the pulpit the evil of contraception had replaced that of insemination, and Hayes the postman once gave Andy more on the subject.

'I know what it is, though there's nothing on the parcel but a Dublin postmark. It's the Pill, that's what it is, and there's more than one couple in the parish receiving it, mind you! The Pill!' repeated Hayes, pronouncing it almost as 'pull'. 'Every time taken, yet another lovely child is prevented,' setting his glass of stout on the bar next to the box with the Black Babies on the front. Hayes, who had not seen a sober bed in forty years, scarcely seemed to notice McShane's utter silence on the subject.

As he married two ends of wire to make a single

strand, McShane thought back on his visit in Taylor's kitchen. For a moment he even considered inviting the American into his own that evening. Surely the writer would enjoy 'The Answer Man' as much as the farmer did? Fridays without fail Andy at 9 p.m. would turn on the old wireless whose square dial in its wooden cabinet gave off a muted golden glow, something about its light comforting him like a cottage window on a winter's night. Seated there he would listen to the Answer Man, who broadcast from a ship somewhere off the English coast. At sea in order to avoid licensing regulations, Radio Gibraltar described itself as a pirate station, bringing to Andy's mind the incongruous image of a Jolly Roger flying from transmitting antennae.

Regardless, he rarely missed the weekly programme whose host responded to questions sent in from all over England and Ireland, Scotland and Wales. No matter the query the Answer Man lived up to his name, supplying listeners with the altitude of any mountain, the distance to the moon and back, the depth of the sea at whatever point, as well as the records of the greatest champions who ever lived. His audience was encouraged to send their questions to a postal address in Gibraltar from which the station took its name.

In all his years of listening Andy had sent in but one question. WHY DO THE SWISS ... he printed in uneven lettering, having his brother-in-law post the letter from Donegal Town so that all Glenmalin need not know of his correspondence with Gibraltar. The Answer Man used it within a fortnight, leading Andy to think it had been an exceptionally good submission. The answer—that they yodel to keep evil spirits from their herd—pleased McShane as well, causing him to reflect that ragwort poisonous to cattle in Ireland was once considered a 'gentle' flower, one favoured by the faeries.

The radio programme made mention of many lands, citing Swaziland with the highest birth-rate in the world; Argentina, home of horses only twenty-eight inches tall; Madagascar with its tenrec, an insectivorous mammal capable of breeding at three weeks of age. As he had with the Swiss herdsmen, McShane would try to square the information with his own experience, wondering if the Andean antiplano described one week were anything at all like the mountain behind his cottage where they cut the turf. Surely it, too, was a bleak enough place on a winter's day: the wind from the north and the grass stiff with frost, a thin sheet of ice on the black pools which filled up where the turf had already been taken.

Mention of the Boer War one evening recalled for Andy a story his father often told. A neighbour had served with the English in South Africa, a man named Ned O'Rourke who enlisted with a cousin named McGinty. As O'Rourke told it, the two of them were one night in a trench on the Transvaal when a great shell struck, taking McGinty's head from his body. As the head passed in front of Ned, it spoke to him going by. 'Goodbye, Ned,' it said. 'Say a prayer for me.'

'Good morning,' said Taylor who had come down the meadow with his fishing pole.

'Dull day,' McShane replied, acknowledging not only the arrival of his neighbour but the clouds also that by now had overcast the sun.

'Well, maybe I'll have better luck.'

'Aye, you might,' Andy said, recognizing his own counsel on fishing conditions bestowed on the Yank a fortnight earlier. When Taylor asked might he purchase a pint of milk as he had done on occasion, McShane explained that the cow now scarcely gave him and Mary enough for their own needs. Forgetting to ask the visitor about cats in heat, he proceeded to tell Taylor of the visit by the technician from the Ministry of Agriculture.

'What if she didn't take?' Taylor asked when Andy finished.

'They will return then, until she does,' McShane replied. 'Sure you can't always tell with those things,' he added, reminded of another visitor years back who rented the shopkeeper's cottage for a holiday. The visitor had some fine breed of a dog along, so that Andy, whose bitch was in heat at the time, kept his own dog locked up in the byre for days, thinking of the grand pups possible if sired by such a specimen. The visitor would walk his dog on a lead, but one afternoon the dog broke free, making like a bullet for Andy's byre. Yet when Andy freed the bitch, she wouldn't let him near.

'Aye, she'd tumble with Paddy's mutt down in the ditch, yet stand there snarling at royalty!'

'What kind was it? Taylor inquired.

'A Malamute,' replied McShane who'd never seen another, though he learned years later from the Answer Man that the breed was named for an Eskimo tribe of Alaska.

From animal husbandry their talk turned to various styles of capital punishment, leading next to the atrocities of war. Was it true McShane asked that the Japanese cut out the tongues of their prisoners during World War II?

'Not with all of them anyhow, because I've an uncle they captured who can talk your ear off yet,' Taylor in a display of wit that startled even himself. At that the two men parted, the Yank heading for the sea, McShane back up to his cottage to tie a fly with the coarse white hairs of the cow's tail salvaged off the barbed wire.

That evening found McShane before the hearth with a newspaper across his knees, a faint hum from the radio all that remained of the pirate station. He sat alone, Mary having departed early to bed as was her custom; the Answer Man having provided his customary share of enlightenment: exposing the people of Iceland as the greatest consumers of refined sugar in the world, later to reveal the gestation period of an Asian elephant as twenty months or more. The broadcast, however, had failed to lift his spirits as it often did.

Still seated, he heard the wind lift round the cottage, rattling the kitchen window. Earlier that week he had been reading late when the wind rose, both suddenly and sharply. Setting aside his book McShane had gone down to the meadow—to run from tramcock to tramcock, anchoring their tops against the wind with heavy stones. Running in the dark without a thought to his footing in the drain-filled field, every inch of which he had come to know since childhood, moving as confidently as another man might across his bedroom floor at night.

Though he'd returned to the cottage with a

sense of elation that other evening, home from an adventure of sorts, its recollection now only depressed him further, the memory gone sour on him like milk left out on a summer's night. Rising, he turned off the wireless; then stepped out to find the wind had swept the clouds away, the waves in the bay below breaking white with the light of the moon.

Still the splendour of the scene merely heightened his despair, though not a soul was there to enquire its source—whether the Japanese prisoners of war, the starving black babies of Africa, or the family that he and Mary had never raised. He heard the voice from the radio programme playing on in his head, as if to echo the futility of facts that raise more questions than they answer. Nor were facts and figures, numbers and names, any antidote for the loneliness that can fill a life. Looking over at Taylor's cottage McShane saw no lights at all.

Might he have done better to know of no other lands than this? he suddenly wondered, staring down at the pasture where he'd run on a moonless night. And no other knowledge either—beyond that red thread on a fly brings the mackerel, and grey crows at springtime herald the arrival of a lamb whose afterbirth they will feed upon. Despite the pressure in his chest, his heart had not betrayed him, his eyes had remained entirely dry. Yet his hands had been ceaselessly working all the while, kneading and twisting relentlessly, so that looking down he saw the newspaper that he had carried out with him—hanging now entirely shredded within his grasp.

Housebound

A month after his mother sold the house, tired as she was of living alone, Brian found himself hired on to a work crew that would disembowel his childhood home. At first only the architects new to the neighbourhood had renovated, much as physicians might heal themselves. Then lawyers and bank officers began to sub-contract as well, scraping out the interiors of their homes as if the houses were only so much old fruit.

The house itself stood on the corner of a wide avenue served by a city bus which began its run in the college square two miles away. For years the neighbourhood had been one largely of city workers, police and fire-fighters, largely Irish-Catholic. In the last few years however, many of the public servants had left, the homes they had rented sold to the newcomers: young professionals, as if white collar were no longer dressy enough.

Unlike Brian's old neighbourhood the east end of the city had held its own, immigrants from the Azores having moved into its tenements as the Italians had done years before. Well known for its University, the chemical industry and chocolate plant below the east end usually surprised those visitors to the city who ever ventured beyond the tall elms and old brick of the college yard. The black neighbourhood between the river and college square had changed little also, and it was on its edge that Brian now lived, sharing a house with two men and two women.

Two of the household were vegetarian; one had attended the University; three of them did not smoke. None of them, however, was free of vice—which made living together easy enough. Brian had given up cigarettes along with teaching grade school, ate poultry but little beef, and every morning now rose to return to his former neighbourhood, like a homeward angel, passing St. Peter's with its white steeple half a mile up the avenue from the old house. It was early spring and the mornings were cool.

The first day on the job he stood in the hallway on the second floor, hammer in hand and plaster at his feet, the exposed laths of the passageway like a skeleton buried in the wall, one too large for the family closets where tradition has assigned them. Or for the kitchen table where every three months or so Uncle Jerry had appeared.

'Where's Jera?' his mother would inquire one morning at breakfast, doing nothing to lighten his father's mood whose sombreness seemed part and parcel of the uniform that even captain's bars in the later years did little to brighten. His father would curtly cut her off, but skilfully working on him, she'd announce a few days later as he left for the police station, 'Tonight you bring your brother home.'

That night Jeremiah would arrive, sixteen

sheets to nowhere, his clothes a filthy mess. 'Are you not your brother's keeper,' came the taunt each time, 'and he but a public inebriate!'

'You're nothing but a street drunk!' shot back his father at the figure following his wife up to draw a bath while Brian took the clothes down to the furnace. Even after he outgrew the notion that bloodied bones lay behind paint cans and paraphernalia stored above the stairs, the descent was never an easy one. The steps slippery, the damp smell of the cellar far stronger than the dim light from a single bulb below.

Dressed in his brother's clothes, Jerry would spend two weeks at their house drying out, feeding on his favourite dishes that his sister-in-law served up as part of the cure. The winter Brian turned thirteen his uncle died, body blasted far beyond his forty-five years of age.

His recollection of Jeremiah was only the first of many that working on the old house elicited. Images long dormant now burst into memory, like flame struck from a book of matches lying untouched for years in some bureau drawer. Replacing a sash in what had been his bedroom, he recalled hours spent gazing at that window, afternoon sunlight behind a green window shade creating a night sky of constellations across its worn and cracked fabric.

The corner of an empty room summoned forth furniture his mother had long since disposed of, a brown easy chair whose tag threatening fines and imprisonment for its removal he had torn off one afternoon, wondering if his father would find out. Evenings his father would fall asleep there, coins from his pockets collecting beneath the cushion where Brian later retrieved them, a seeming multitude of sins to surround a single chair.

After a fortnight two Irish lads arrived to begin the plastering. They were a few years younger than Brian, in their early twenties. Not long over from Ireland, they came from the same county as his great-grandfather. Although they talked some with Brian of their time in the States, he did not share with them his relationship to the house. Puzzling over his reticence, he remembered a story told by Uncle Jerry, of Irish labourers who refused to level the Indian burial mounds on a construction site somewhere in the Mid-West. Still, it seemed he hardly risked the wrath of ancient spirits here: at most whatever memories were released in the razing of the rooms.

All the same he found himself often uneasy in the house. At odds with his ambivalence, he wondered if it involved his mother's move into an apartment complex for the elderly. Were he a truly Irish son, unmarried as he was, he would yet live with his mother, a situation which seemed to Brian as strange an arrangement as the two Irish might find his own communal household.

Walking to the corner store at lunchtime he sometimes ran into those his age who had never left the neighbourhood. Their faces startled him, at once foreign and familiar, eyes sunken, the finer features now swollen, edges grown fat or begun to curl. Never to leave was apparently no way to get back home either he decided—as though Michael Kenny limping from an auto accident years before, or his brother Bobby with more than a little furniture missing, were not alone among the somehow maimed whom he encountered there.

Though he would not meet Danny Mahan, Brian often thought of his closest friend who had lived five doors down in a larger home whose garage was a converted carriage house. Danny had indeed moved on, first to the University itself, then to Alaska to homestead, as logical a progression as Brian's turn to carpentry three years out of teacher's college.

Even as a kid Danny had ranged further afield, leading Brian on bike across the city into the University neighbourhood where quieter streets met on curves rather than at right angles. Over several falls they ran from a thin man with a foreign accent who chased them from the towering horse chestnut in his yard, then one day lured them into the barn behind his house. Once there, he lectured them on the physics of sonar, shooting worms from a spring-loading pistol at the bats which swooped among the rafters. Back at the loft behind Danny's house they fashioned experiments of their own: cigarettes, theoretical sex, and once some sherry that threw their stomachs off.

'It happened before you two were born. Before your family bought the place, Danny,' Delaney the postman told them once, pointing back at the carriage house. 'The foundation had begun to cave in at the back, so they jacked the whole thing up to drive new posts into the cellar. They were lowering the entire frame when a supporting beam slipped, pinning one of the two boogies on the job.'

'Was he hurt bad?' they asked.

'Oh, that nigger was pretty well crushed,' Delaney

replied, the epithets even then seeming to Brian utterly at odds with the detailed account of a man's death. Now fifteen years later he knew his present address by the river, if not Alaska, was tantamount to Africa for the Delaneys young and old along the avenue.

It was not long after Brian heard the story of the black man that his Uncle Jeremiah died. A year later his father, near to St. Patrick's Day. Delivering the mail around noon, Delaney spoke briefly with the captain who was working a night shift. His mother had gone shopping that morning, to return shortly before Brian came home from school. She found her husband in the brown easychair—asleep she thought, until seeing the cigarette burned down to his fingers.

'There's been an accident,' she told Brian, who could only think of the argument that morning over his failure to sweep out the cellar. 'Never let the sun set on your anger,' advised the Gospel, but then God had not even waited on sundown.

A late snow fell the night before the funeral, drawing a white sheet over the neighbourhood by morning. Standing on the front porch he watched the limousine that would take them to St. Peter's approach, to brake suddenly as though genuflecting, the snow on its hood falling softly onto the street in front. More than his father's name uttered among the Latin phrases, it was for Brian the mass of blue uniforms within the church that finally brought the death home, his complicity assured by the judge among the mourners who slipped a ten-dollar bill into his hand as they followed the casket out.

Another week passed and the clutter outside the

house grew. A blue dumpster parked in the driveway overflowed with the skin and bones of the old rooms. Cartons of Italian tiles with instructions in French lay beneath scaffolding at the back, awaiting completion of an upstairs bath whose ceiling they fitted with straight-grain fir. His mother had sold to a man at the University, but there would be no bats in his belfry, computer sciences, not sonar, his field of study.

The renovation had Brian's mother baffled. Disapproving of all, she might in time have reconciled herself to a wood stove in the front room, or even to the solar collectors on the southern roof. Taken together however, such changes seemed to her much like someone trying to walk in two directions simultaneously. Stopping by the house one afternoon, she told Brian that his great-grandfather had worked at carpentry upon first arriving from Ireland. If her meaning were that he'd never been lucky enough to teach for a living, she kept to herself her disappointment on this score.

Upon hindsight he saw clearly enough the shadows cast that morning of the accident to come. The sidewalk on his way to work littered with earthworms: having surfaced to escape rainwater the previous evening, they now risked drowning in the puddles left by the storm. Nearing the corner he saw a sheet of black plastic across the attic window sucked in like a sunken cheek upon the face of the house.

Unlike his childhood fear, no ceiling—above his bed or otherwise—fell down on him. Rather, they were at work in his parents' bedroom on the second floor, installing a sliding door which would open onto a new deck built above the back porch. The door stood where two windows had been enlarged and joined, creating a glass wall with one partition that slid along a metal track.

After an hour they had the door manoeuvred into place, only it refused to slide. Kneeling at the open end, Brian pulled while two others pushed. The door remained jammed, debris or a pebble lodged among the rollers, but what came free was a scene from a night in that room twenty years before. His father away at work when his mother woke him, leading him still half-asleep into her bedroom where the drawn-up shades made the windows even larger than life. Through the bare trees he saw a moon that seemed to consume itself in the shadow moving slowly across its face.

Trapped in a flood of memory he barely managed to draw back his head as the door jumped its track, slamming six inches past its scheduled stop to pin his right hand against the wall. Through the unbroken pane he stared still half-asleep at the blood from his lacerated fingers, spreading slowly across the glass like some outsized laboratory slide. He felt no pain as yet, only a certain sense of relief; knowing that if nothing more than their combined efforts had sprung that door, he was done with the house. 'Dangerous to be safe in here,' remarked Uncle Jerry often, delighting his nephew with paradox as he stumbled against a kitchen chair.

He remained kneeling while the two Irish prised the door out, releasing the hand which he examined just long enough to be startled by something white in the bloody tear across the inner knuckles. Walking slowly to a waiting car he noticed as acutely as though taking inventory, a ball of marking twine, bent nails, and a beer can, sawdust scattered across the mud of the trampled yard.

'You're lucky, you know,' a doctor informed him at the hospital, dividing his attention between Brian and a drunk brought in by the police with a gash across his forehead. 'Another quarter of an inch, and you'd be maimed, my friend,' he added, his tone full of a satisfaction that surgeons, like carpenters, can find in fractions. An inch as good as a mile in a man's nose, according to Jeremiah.

'You're lucky, you know,' a neighbour with dubious tact told his mother a month after his father died. 'If that cigarette hadn't gone out, you'd have also lost the house.'

Well, he was rid of the house at last he knew, though not through fire, nor by tearing it apart room by room, as if looking for an exit. Even as a child, he remembered now, he had rearranged those rooms: not with a wrecking bar, but by moving with a mirror held level at his chin so that looking down where the floor belonged he walked along the ceiling, stepping high over walls that vanished no matter how quickly he removed the mirror to glance at his feet. Seated on the edge of the examining table, he decided that if the way out had proved the way back, it was probably just as well—because there was no escaping that path, as surely as the stitches along his fingers would be scar within the week, the very tissue of memory for this day in years to come.

He was free to go, a nurse told him, if not to Alaska or Ireland just this week, at least back to his neighbourhood by the river. Since the hospital lay to the north of the city, he walked home past the University, feeling the air still fresh from the previous night's rain. The streets were lined with maples, the sidewalks thick with their tiny yellow flowers. Like plaster dust he decided, scattered across the city.

Of Saints And Scholars

'You're the very man for the job,' offered Maguire in a half-whisper, leaning so near that McElliot could only note how much like single buckshot his pupils were, fired into the centre of the iris. So small he surely had difficulty with the dark.

McElliot said nothing, his mind racing on to head Maguire off. Whether smuggling butter South or running sugar North, he knew his man Maguire who only last month had lost a finger. One story said throwing bombs into the river after salmon; a different version that after selling the fish to a local guesthouse, he shot the finger off hunting rabbit. Either way the man was a chancer, a hustler, a bucko. Were he political in any way as well, McElliot could not say.

'Myself the man?' he did say, cautiously.

'Aye,' said Maguire in the same hushed voice. 'I've a great idea for a story.'

A dubious scheme all the same McElliot reflected, though less likely to lead them down bog roads at midnight, headlamps dimmed. Yet if relieved, he felt flattered also. Of all plots offered authors by waitresses and taxi-men, Maguire's proposition was McElliot's first.

It was the writer's fifth summer in Donegal, stopping at an old cottage purchased with the cheque from an American magazine that paid beyond belief. If he had yet to sell that crowd a second story, the cottage welcoming him each July sustained in McElliot an abiding, albeit seasonal, flush of success. What was more, he did well enough with the locals. Born in Dublin, he had travelled and lived abroad, no doubt seemed more a visitor than Irish to his neighbours. The village itself, blessed with magnificent mountains tumbling to the sea, saw a great deal of visitors during the good months. In recent years, almost as many as during those grand summers, innumerable tourist coaches, before the Troubles started up across the Border sixty miles east.

That McElliot wrote for a living made little impact on his neighbours—until the past winter when a story appeared in a Dublin paper. A harmless tale, it recounted the feud between two brothers which brought them both before the court. The bare bones of the story McElliot had exhumed from a provincial paper down South, Kerry or Cork, but the setting was obviously Glenmore, only thinly disguised, and the villagers had passed the paper around.

'Written by the fellow who owns Watty's place,' they informed those who hadn't McElliot's name.

When he returned to Glenmore that summer, the author sensed a certain shift in the wind. 'God bless you, Mr. McElliot,' intoned Bernard Carr whenever the two men met, never failing to remind McElliot of some favour done the writer on his first visit to the glen. 'It wouldn't do to leave *you* standing there,' remarked a neighbour who now stopped to lift McElliot on the road into the shops. Cautious in most things, the writer had never learned to drive.

McElliot himself liked to fancy the favouring breeze sprang from a lingering trace of that ancient respect for the wandering bard. Like a good deal of respect, a consideration founded greatly on fear. Spurned, a poet might retaliate in verse and rhyme, dubious imitations of immortality his revenge. God bless you to leave me out of your stories seemed to be Bernard's plea.

Being only human McElliot found some pleasure in all of this, found himself turning toward Maguire with greater warmth.

'A story is it?'

'Aye,' said Maguire, wasting no time. 'A woman mad with religion. Killing children before they reach the age of reason.'

'To make saints of them,' he finished, eyes fixed on McElliot.

Although the writer scarcely nodded, his companion, like a dog encouraged by crumbs, shifted even closer.

'She goes to the rail at every Mass. A daily Communicant, so there's no suspicion on her. She does in a dozen before they're on to her!'

'And how do they get on to her?' McElliot asked, more appalled than flattered by the offerings of Maguire's muse. A faraway memory surfaces somewhere at the back of his head, tales told by the Sisters, of Filipino children tortured by the Japs during the last war. To renounce their faith, the nuns explained, detailing the slivers of bamboo employed by the heathen soldiers.

'Is it the priest?' Maguire queried in turn. Apparently he hadn't this wrinkle worked out as yet. 'He has it from her in confession ... but he can't use that, of course.'

'Maybe in a moment of passion?' he suggested with a leer, wee pupils like ball bearings.

It wouldn't do at all, the editor in McElliot observed to himself. She would scarcely confess if she considered herself to be creating saints. And his man Maguire was making a balls of it, serving up a side-dish of sex along with the murders. An old woman making saints and the Parish Priest both, was it? Too many British tabloids for his companion he could only conclude. The once-banned *New of the World*, solace of the Borstal Boy in English gaols, now flogged outside Irish chapels after Sunday Mass. Telefis Eireann headed rapidly down the same road.

'I doubt that kind of writing would go down well in Ireland,' he told Maguire with a laugh, half-surprised at his own prudishness.

'Not to worry! It's all EEC at the moment, the Common Market. No problem at all, at all!'

'Well, you should get on with it, so.'

'I couldn't write home!' Maguire said. If annoyed, not fooled in the least by McElliot's seeming obtuseness. 'I'm nothing with words, only I'm giving you the idea.'

'And is it your own?' McElliot asked, a hint of the law colouring his tone, as if copyright were suddenly his sole concern.

'It is, indeed,' Maguire said. '"Sure they're

saints in Heaven," remarks the wife the day three children perish by fire near Killarney. Gives me the idea her self, she does. It's automatic, you know, if you're under seven years of age.' In a helpful tone, should there be points of doctrine as well as law that might be holding the writer back.

Like a free pass into the pictures McElliot mused; only better, to hear Maguire tell it. 'It would be handy all right,' he said aloud for the other's benefit. 'Save all the bother, expense of Canonization.' Unearthing miracles, sending petitions to Rome. Never mind countless prayers to Heaven. Did they still engage an *Advocatus Diaboli* he wondered?

Only last summer Ireland had celebrated the canonization of Blessed Oliver. What McElliot chiefly remembered was Papal praise of Plunkett —drawn, quartered, and beheaded—as 'a model of reconciliation'. No doubt he had obeyed like a corpse, as the Jesuits asked of their own. Perhaps it was all best apprehended through irony, approached as one would Matt Talbot's Bar in Boston, named for the reformed-alchoholic Dublin ascetic, even now rumoured to be Ireland's next saint. A dive full of rugby players dancing to a rock and roll band the evening McElliot had dropped in. Not a hairshirt to be seen or felt.

Irony, however, was not a strong suit of Matt Maguire. No subtle shifts or unexpected turns (unless possibly down a bog road to beat the law) need apply here. Nothing but the strong sell. 'We could flesh it out, I suppose,' McElliot offered accordingly. 'A chapter for every manner of demise. One for drowning, another for poison.' The entire undertaking of a sudden so unreal that he gave in utterly to his collaborator, suggesting suffocation and dismemberment as if they were wallpaper patterns.

'There you are!' shouted Maguire, catching a glimpse of his own genius in the mirror of McElliot's enthusiasm. 'Film rights and more!' he ejaculated, caught up in the flush.

'And your interest in it?' the literary agent in McElliot asked.

'Twenty-five per cent.'

'I thought it was running butter you were about,' the writer confided in a confidential tone.

'Ach, the fecking Common Market has put an end to that,' Maguire groused. 'No bloody money to be made in groceries now at all.'

It was high time to get down to work again, McElliot told himself on the road home. His latest story, a day in the life of a Madrid museum guard, finished over a month ago. Though he hadn't enlightened Maguire on the subject, the story the village had seen that winter was his first ever set in Ireland. The majority unfolded rather in locales like Amsterdam or San Francisco, even Athens and Istanbul. All a good distance from Glenmore, nor was it a matter of miles alone.

Still for all the absurdity of Maguire's yarn, there was in McElliot's work a contrasting lack of imagination. A sense of something missing which was at best only partially obscured by the foreign, sometimes exotic setting. Editors who praised his eye for detail cited the absence of something else, putting words on it ranging from 'conflict' to 'compulsion'. No one went so far as to accuse him of substituting topography for inspiration, however, and surely he sold enough work to be considered successful in a modest way. More money than in groceries at any rate, he chuckled to himself, pausing at his gate to note the moonlight like spotlamps on sheep in the park below.

The memory of Maguire's mad woman tagged after McElliot the next day, like a headache from too much drink. There was correspondence to answer, a few clothes to wash, nothing demanding enough to bar the mind's door entirely against her. Passing up the pub that evening he began a murder mystery purchased in the shop next to the Chapel.

By the following day McElliot could see her features as clearly as if he had dreamt them. She was no caricature as Maguire might have drawn her, all streaming hair and frantic eyes. Rather her face was on the long side, though short of horsy, the flesh still firm for her age which McElliot gauged to be somewhere over seventy. Short in stature, she stood slightly stooped at the shoulder, dressed in a black skirt with a scarlet cardigan over a black top. The skirt was dusty with turf ash, the sweater worn through at the elbows.

She appeared the next morning in the same outfit which he guessed she probably wore for days on end. He wondered now if that were how long she intended to stay on, grateful she was at least the silent type. Unable to work, he began another paperback detective, not a female over twenty-five in its world of crime.

Boiling an egg for his tea that evening McElliot managed a closer look, remarking in her eyes perhaps the first clue to her condition. It was nothing as facile as a demented gaze: more a flicker of real pain beneath depths of sadness, like the glimmer of goldfish at the bottom of a garden pool. Or was the simile itself too much a garden variety, he mused—before recoiling with a start that suggested his fish had metaphorized into something worse.

There was no need at all for tropes of any kind he shouted aloud. Nor would he write a word of it down. She was Maguire's woman, not his, and it was obvious she had worn her welcome out. If McElliot had been initially curious it had been in a suitably professional manner, as disinterested as any doctor with a patient. With no intention of a story, however, the process had become somewhat akin to eavesdropping, though she had yet to utter a single word. More like peering through a window at an old woman—a practice likely to prove more distasteful yet.

Halfway through his egg he saw her latest appearance offered him a clue to her origins. Above her mouth he had spied a small mole with several whiskers, resembling a birthmark on his sister's face. Summoning the old woman to mind, he remarked this time a likeness in the line of her brow to his other sister. As recognition of the familiar upon daybreak lightens a nightmare's dread, a relieved McElliot saw that the face was composed to some degree of features borrowed from his older siblings, executed in the fashion of a composite police sketch used to identify perpetrators of violent crime. Juxtaposing this nose with that moustache until the victim has his man.

Having espied the familiar, even familial, in her physiognomy, McElliot banished the old woman at once. Grateful for their intercession, he would write his sisters in the morning. Answer the card which had annoyed him upon its arrival the previous week, picturing the Swiss Guards at the Vatican in full dress. Annoyed him because it was at least five years since their pilgrimage to Rome where they had apparently purchased a great reserve of postcards.

The cards still tracked McElliot down from time to time, scenes of Michaelangelo's Moses or St. Peter's Square, stamped with the postmark of the small English village near Bristol where they lived. It was not the Italian art which irritated him. More its ecclesiastical content, his sisters having grown increasingly religious over the years, as if to compensate for his own drift from the Church. To McElliot their cards were too much like notices from his dentist in the post, colourful reminders of the Divine Appointments made on his behalf.

The latest card told of a trip to London for a rally. How moving it had been: 100,000 gathered there; they'd had orange drinks on the train in. They were as vague as that, but McElliot gathered from an English paper left by a visitor in the pub that it had been an anti-abortion protest, though evidently his sisters had been other than conservative in their estimate of the crowd.

'A rally?' he would write them, feigning ignorance. 'I didn't know you were political?' though that wasn't entirely true either. 'You know we have a soft spot in our hearts for Franco,' they wrote him during the dictator's dying days: the stability of Europe for his sisters having little to do with Common Markets or currency links. 'And hasn't he stood like a bastion against Communism for all these years?' they penned on a black and white card of the Catacombs.

At breakfast the old woman was back, dogging McElliot with an authority that sent him fleeing for the dictionary. 'Autochthonous,' he half-remembered aloud, and he was right at that, only confusion as to its spelling had him searching for several minutes. 'Indigenous as in rocks' read the first definition, but it was psychology, not geology, he wanted:

adj. 2. Pertaining to ideas which arise apart from an individual's train of thought, seeming to have some alien or external agency as their source.

He paused at its hint of the subversive, seemingly suggesting his sisters' favourite agents of change, outside agitators and the KGB. Obviously it was not his man Maguire's woman anymore. Nor had his sisters much to do with it as he saw this morning, beyond a few minor details. Even at that he had observed how the woman's upper lip with its mole sometimes quivered. Like a rabbit he thought, something that sister had never resembled.

Neither was it any longer like eavesdropping.

Instead the woman now followed him, from kitchen to scullery to bedroom, managing the step up or down between every room. 'You might at least help with the washing-up,' he told her after dinner, though it was well past the point where feeble humour might set the situation right. Hagiography was not his strong suit; obsession nothing he'd ever cared to tackle in his writing—something better left to the Russians. Unable to work, he wondered if he were not being unravelled by the woman as one would undo a jumper, pulling all the while on a single thread. As if to reassure him the old woman began to knit by an open fire, a faded picture of the Sacred Heart above the hearth.

After supper McElliot took a walk along the strand. Following the ribbon of wrack unwound by the tide, he found his fine eye for detail turned morbid also, descrying nothing but decay in the debris flung up by the sea. Immortality alone in the scraps of coloured plastic which time itself would not touch.

Retrieving a sheep's skull from the sand, he saw the parched membrane of its nasal cavity shift in the wind, sered like an autumn leaf. 'You're in a grand way, lad,' he told himself, turning back.

In the days following McElliot tried to make a story of it after all, settling on Agnes for a name. 'Exorcism of a sort,' he muttered, only it didn't seem to take. Refusing confinement to the typewritten page, Agnes preferred to ghost round the cottage, taking every opportunity to throw herself across the tracks of his train of thought. If Maguire had offered but melodrama for motivation ('mad with religion'), the old woman tried to help McElliot here, speaking out at last.

'Modern times,' she said at breakfast, her host buried in the Dublin paper he bought out of loyalty for the story they had published. ''Tis to save them from times such as these.'

It was of small use to him, her words merely echoing the despair that had washed over the writer since his walk along the strand. As if the morbidity midst wrack and flotsam had come to colour all that he saw, even the daily paper which of late seemed little more than a catalogue of atrocity and deprivation.

That morning's leader told of a small boy killed in Belfast by a letter bomb. Unable to finish the story, he turned to finer type relating the arrival of a major relic at St. Oliver's birthplace. The left femur bone the final paragraph revealed. Of 'Letters to the Editor' he read a lengthy one discounting the hazards of nuclear waste, a shorter letter warning of certain risks to hygiene in licking postage stamps. Though he was not prepared to take a stand on either issue, their juxtaposition evidence enough the world was utterly out of whack.

'It's the age we live in,' she told him again.

It was a start, he supposed, though he knew he wasn't the man for the job. Seated once in the Abbey beside an aged countryman, McElliot had marvelled at how the old fellow recoiled, even groaned aloud whenever the decrepit crone of the production came scolding onstage. The peasant acceptance of the old woman's reality, akin to the credence once granted the Devil in morality plays, left McElliot wishing he might create characters with a similar impact.

Now faced with the task he found himself unequal to it. The years of continental cafés, the foreign capitals—all having rendered him too much a part of modern times, unfit for what seemed almost a medieval undertaking. Lacking even his sister's faith, he knew it would take something stronger than orange drink to look upon the world as Agnes did. It was not healthy or human he held, to take on all the sorrows of creation like that. One wanted to keep the historical perspective in mind. With slots for commercial messages, as in the TV series on the Blacks and Jews he argued, shuddering at the sudden memory of a schoolmate who severed his hand at the wrist one Sunday after Mass. The text that morning Matthew, Chapter V, on casting out the sinning eye.

He was prone of late to violent attacks of memory, as sharp as the bamboo splinters administered in the martyrdom of Filipino youth. Spasms like that which returned him to the morning he arrived first of all scholars to the schoolyard: to find jammed through the doorhandle a dead rabbit, its headless torso twisted there like a rag to stop the draught.

Sunday morning he rose to find his melancholy gone, its dark mood like the heavy swell on a sluggish sea given over to a high wind and racing waves. He tore out of bed to prepare a breakfast large enough for two. To McElliot's eye the tea-ball submerged in the pot resembled a depth charge, setting the water to roil and tumble as the air escaped below. He felt the power of imagination sweeping him along like the California surf, conflict and compulsion as near to hand as the salt and pepper on his breakfast table.

Agnes failed to appear, having slept in he decided. Seated yet at the table, he caught himself calculating ages of the lads and lasses returning from Mass along the road, trying to gauge who was not yet seven. When evening brought no relief he set out for the pub, frightened that he was coming entirely unstuck. As he passed the long meadow sloping seaward from the road, McElliot recalled a Christmas visit to Donegal, a farmer piling turf and straw upon a large rock in the middle of the field, keeping a fire over it day and night so that a bucket of cold water one morning would crack the stone asunder.

Taking a stool beneath the colour television, he ordered a bottle of stout. Bernard Carr came over for a chat, of which McElliot held up his end with surprising success. 'God bless you, Mr. McElliot,' Bernard offered in parting as Maguire came in the door, leaving the writer to think it was himself who had more cause to fear the locals than they him. He watched Maguire settle in beside the fire, next to Mickey the Post. Full of mail-fraud schemes without a doubt.

The television came on above him. Looking up, McElliot felt as if he were underwater, peering at figures in a green sea overhead. The picture focused as the news began, opening with film footage of the funeral that morning in Belfast, the small boy killed by the letter bomb. The camera showed the procession with wee casket down a crowded street, a close-up of mourners on a corner. Suddenly a grey-haired woman filled the screen, lifting her grandson not five years old above her head so that he might see the cortege.

The lad looked simply puzzled, but it was the woman who held McElliot's eye. Her face contorted and she was shouting. The sound was terrible, yet half-reading her lips he heard something about martyrs and saints, the child in her arms beginning to cry. With that the set turned sea-green again and the pub itself began to spin. McElliot grabbed the edge of the bar, holding on until his eyes could focus. Gazing wildly round the room he wondered if Maguire has seen their woman, mad with religion, making saints and martyrs of mere children.

'He must be in the toilet!' he stammered aloud, turning a few heads along the bar. The faces regarding him began to spin, soon joined by others. His two sisters, a likeness of Blessed Oliver from the colour photogravure of a Sunday supplement, the Generalissimo, his best chum from primary school, Maguire putting in an appearance at last, the screaming grandmother from the telly, but no Agnes. 'To be set free by the Nine O'Clock News,' he marvelled, before his head began to whirl so hard he was afraid it would fly apart.

He had no memory of the road home when he rose from bed late the next afternoon. He felt as if he had slept hours—felt utterly exhausted, yet not unfit. A cup of tea taken, he stepped from the cottage into a gentle rain. Noting to himself the sharp edge of turf smoke, acrid against the soft, amorphous air, McElliot knew he was his own man once more. More suited to contrast than conflict, he began that very evening another story. Of an Irishman who had emigrated to New Zealand. A lover of flowers, he cross-bred and perfected countless hybrids, trying for years to create a perfectly black rose. Time and time again a black bud formed, only to have a crimson stain seep always in as the petals slowly blossomed.

For full deails of all Poolbeg Press books in print, write to

Poolbeg Press,
Knocksedan House,
Swords, Co. Dublin.
Telephone 401133.
Telex 24639.

ANTHONY CRONIN

DEAD AS DOORNAILS

THE LIVELIEST, LOVELIEST MEMOIR OF BEHAN, MYLES & KAVANAGH EVER WRITTEN

In the first half of this century, Dublin was the stage across which many of the most magical names in Irish and world literature trod — Joyce, Yeats, Stephens, Gogarty, O'Casey were but a handful. We may sometimes feel that with the dawning of the century's second half, these days had gone forever. Such a view, however, is probably induced by our not being distanced enough from these more recent times to perceive their enchantment. For enchantment they had — enchantment aplenty — with such personalities, now almost legendary, as Brendan Behan, Myles na Gopaleen, and Patrick Kavanagh enriching the scene. It was a scene Anthony Cronin knew intimately — indeed helped to create — and the narrative of his exploits and exchanges with these and other fabulous creatures has justly gained its reputation as one of the greatest chronicles of its kind. With its combination of wild humour and heart-stirring pathos it is as invaluable a record as it is imperishable a memoir. It has the stamp of a masterpiece.

0 905169 31 X/110x178mm/308pp/April/Paper £1.75

A LIFE OF HER OWN

Maeve Kelly

". . . richly human and perceptive and highly recommended to all those who have not yet had the pleasure." *Sunday Press.*

0 905169 04 2/110x178mm/144pp/Paper/£1.50

A GIFT HORSE

Kate Cruise O'Brien

"I am going to stick my neck out, and possibly make a fool of myself. It is a thing that even the most conservative critic has to do once or twice in a lifetime. It is unarguable that Kate Cruise O'Brien's stories reveal a very special talent, but each time I reread them, and I have now read them three times, I get the feeling that they reveal something much more — a seed of genius."
Sunday Press

"These stories slide themselves into the best of company and are rewardingly full of promise."
Irish Press

0 905169 08 5/184x112mm/128pp/Paper/£1.50